STO

KEY TO THE PAST

The Hamiltons were a clannish family. No outsider dared to intrude on their grief when the much-loved Randall met his death in a road accident. Yet the girl who came unexpectedly to Hamilton House one dark, wintry night had reason to hate and despise the dead man — and her visit was the key to the past with its burden of guilt. Kyre Hamilton, the head of the family, learned that conscience had indeed made cowards of many . . .

JULIET GRAY

KEY TO THE PAST

Complete and Unabridged

LINFORD
Leicester

First published in Great Britain

First Linford Edition
published 1999

British Library CIP Data

Gray, Juliet, *1933 –*
    Key to the past.—Large print ed.—
Linford romance library
    1. Love stories
    2. Large type books
    I. Title
    823.9′14 [F]

ISBN 0–7089–5528–2

Published by
F. A. Thorpe (Publishing) Ltd.
Anstey, Leicestershire

Set by Words & Graphics Ltd.
Anstey, Leicestershire
Printed and bound in Great Britain by
T. J. International Ltd., Padstow, Cornwall

This book is printed on acid-free paper

1

The grey sky invested the countryside with a bleak, forbidding gloom. The tall trees, divested of their summer foliage, were gaunt and stark against the backcloth of an overcast sky. A cold and blustery wind tossed the spattering rain hither and thither and the small cluster of houses and farms seemed to huddle closer to the earth for warmth and protection.

Although it was early evening, darkness was on its way and Sara tried to quicken her faltering steps as she bowed her tired body against the wind. She was cold and weary and she drew her damp coat closer about her, thankful that she had almost reached the end of her long journey.

Pain shuddered through her body and she paused, waiting for it to abate, looking upwards to the big house which stood in quiet dignity on the brow of the hill in proud defiance of the elements . . .

Within that big house all was warmth and comfort and the evidence of wealth. The wind and rain battered in vain at the strong, sturdy walls. Log fires roared in the huge chimneys: thick carpets hugged floors from wall to wall; heavy velvet curtains were drawn against the wintry day and the fury outside was scarcely heard in the quiet study.

Long legs stretched to the warmth of the fire, a book within easy reach, a pipe going well and his favourite spaniel with her head on his knee, Kyre Hamilton gazed into the flickering flames. Idly and absently, he caressed the silken, floppy ears of the dog whose adoring, unblinking gaze never left his face.

He was a quiet man and he appreciated the peace and the intimacy of this evening hour. His thoughts were still attuned to the recent work on the new book and he was suffused with content and the knowledge of a good day's work behind him. He mulled over the next chapter, his quick brain leaping ahead to form phrases and to evolve a neat turn of dialogue. A writer of historical novels, he loved to dwell on the days of the eighteenth century . . . days of romance, of adventure, of history . . . days of poverty and misery and ignorance . . . days that he could bring to life again with his brilliant pen.

Tall, dark-haired and dark-eyed, his features bore the undeniable stamp of the Hamiltons — straight, aristocratic nose, a firm, slightly autocratic chin, sensual yet oddly sensitive mouth. He was not handsome but there was a certain magnetism about his looks that had its own appeal. Quiet-spoken, firm yet compassionate, distinguished yet blessed with a natural humility, he was a man of integrity and honour.

The logs shifted and sparks flew and he roused from his drowsy reverie. He straightened in his comfortable arm-chair with its high, winged back and was conscious of stiffness and a

3

pleasant sleepiness.

Even as he roused, the door opened on the sound of light voices and a faint resentment touched his eyes briefly. But he smiled a welcome as he turned in his chair to greet the invaders of his solitude.

Cathryn Hamilton moved with so much youth, so much eager vitality that she almost danced. Her dark, curling hair rioted all over the small, well-shaped head. Her dark, sparkling eyes were full of merriment and an enchanting eagerness. Her well-cut, aristocratic features bore the Hamilton stamp in a softer, feminine mould. Her linen dress emphasised the youthful curves of a slim, straight body.

'In the dark, Kyre?' It was her companion who spoke and switched on the main light so that he blinked a little in the flood of brightness.

'We thought you were working — but I guess we've caught you napping by the fire!' There was a lilt of laughter, of mocking accusation, in Cathryn's voice

4

as she came to perch on the arm of his chair. She smiled at him with affectionate warmth. 'Are we trampling on your dreams, darling?'

He smiled. 'Dreams? A pastime of the young and the innocent, Cathryn. My youth and my innocence have vanished with the years — and so have my dreams, I'm afraid.'

Honor moved to warm her hands at the fire and he drew in his long legs to make room. She looked down at him, one eyebrow raised in cool amusement. 'Is this a new rôle?'

He looked up at her. 'Rôle?'

'The cynic.'

'Oh . . . I'm not a cynic except in the sense that I accept human nature as it is and refuse to be shocked or disappointed or surprised by anything that people do or say,' he returned lightly. He went on evenly: 'I'm not in the habit of dreaming in the firelight because I haven't the time or the inclination to indulge in wild fantasies. I was thinking about the new book.'

'Which is based, no doubt, on little more than wild fantasy,' she pointed out, smiling.

'My books are based on historical fact,' he amended quietly. 'The fantasy is introduced for the benefit of those who like a little light relief with their history.'

'How is the book going?' Cathryn twined her fingers in his crisp, dark hair.

Gently but firmly he pushed away her hand. 'Well enough.'

'Cautious Kyre!' she jeered, wrinkling her pretty nose at him. 'You never give anything away, do you?'

He smiled. 'Have you had a good day?' He turned the subject, hating to discuss his work with anyone until a book was completed and he could feel that he had done his best and its fate rested with his publishers and his readers.

'Not bad. We ran into Colin Hammond in Regent Street.'

'Not literally, I hope.'

She laughed. 'The car was parked at

the time. I've invited Colin to dinner next week — he's coming to stay with his parents for a few days.'

He nodded. 'Good.'

She went on lightly: 'This weather is foul. I do hate driving in wet weather.'

'Because you will drive too fast,' Honor said with faint disapproval. 'These narrow lanes are treacherous in the rain.'

Unabashed, she retorted blithely: 'Well, I brought you back in one piece, didn't I? I'm perfectly safe at the wheel. I've been driving since I was old enough to have a licence!'

'Such a long time ago,' Kyre teased gently.

'Four years,' she retorted defensively. 'With nary an accident to date — nor even the hint of one.' Almost unconsciously, her fingers sought the curved edge of the low table.

'Randall used to boast that he was safe at the wheel, too,' Honor said quietly.

A shadow leaped swiftly to Cathryn's

eyes and Kyre stiffened involuntarily at the calm, unfeeling words.

'Not very tactful, Honor,' he said coldly. 'No one knows what actually happened that day ... there's no evidence that Randall was driving too fast and he knew these roads like the back of his hand.'

'I'm sorry, darling,' she murmured. 'I'm only trying to impress on Cathryn that accidents happen so easily.'

Those dark, lively eyes blazed with fierce anger for the Hamiltons were cursed with a swift, hot temper and an impetuosity that often led to regret. 'Do you really think that I need to be reminded?' she demanded with a coldness that belied the heat of her anger. 'Do you think that any of us can forget Randall's death so easily?'

'My dear Cathryn, of course not ... but remembering doesn't seem to curb your own love of speed,' Honor said smoothly.

Cathryn leaped to her feet. 'This is a depressing conversation! Let's drink to the future and forget the past.' Her tone was gay, careless. 'Sherry, Honor?'

Kyre noticed the disapproval in Honor's eyes, the sudden tightness of her mouth. The gaiety of his cousin's tone, the swift lithe movement, did not deceive the man who knew her so well. It had been tactless, even cruel of Honor to speak of Randall in that particularly slighting manner. It almost amounted to a taunt. Randall had been young, reckless, full of life and laughter but he had never been careless or irresponsible. He had been a capable, careful motorist and Kyre did not believe that his death was due to any fault in his handling of that small car which had been so badly wrecked. It was an inexplicable accident and the loss was still too recent for careless, thoughtless mention.

Cathryn had been deeply attached to her brother. They had been firm friends and enjoyed a closeness that seldom exists between brother and sister. All the family had felt Randall's death very much — but it had been the greater loss for Cathryn, already bereft of both parents.

One did not mourn for ever, of course: they had all realised that it would be wrong to avoid any mention of Randall or the accident. But it had been a cruel whim of fate to snatch a handsome and lovable young man from the life he loved so much. The family talked of him often when they were alone: remembered his escapades, his love of practical jokes, his quick wit and easy laughter, his intelligence and understanding, the hot temper that flared so swiftly and cooled so quickly, the all-embracing warmth and generosity of his nature. They did not want to forget Randall.

But at Honor's words it seemed that Kyre and Cathryn Hamilton drew closer together and barred her from the intimate confines of the family grief.

Kyre looked steadily at the tall, superbly beautiful woman as she sipped her sherry. The harsh thrust of light did not mar the beauty of those classical, cooly serene features nor shadow those velvety, challenging eyes. Her glossy hair was drawn from the nape of her neck in a sleek chignon, a hint of blue in its raven depths. Her simple yet sophisticated dress was not designed to emphasise the lovely moulding of her body yet subtly conveyed the exciting, sense-stirring appeal of a woman who was desirable in the eyes of men.

Kyre met those dark eyes — and wondered at the coldness in himself that could not be stirred to warmth by her undeniable beauty and the magnetism of her charm and the affection that she did not conceal. He knew that everyone, including Honor herself, expected him to marry her eventually — and perhaps he would . . . one day. But he was in no hurry to take a wife until he had been fully convinced that love and all its complications was not likely to enter his life . . .

Honor Pattison moved uncomfortably beneath his steady, contemplative gaze, wondering at the thoughts which lurked behind that attractive face which gave away so few secrets. One could seldom guess at Kyre's thoughts and he was perhaps the only man who could cause her self-possession to falter.

These Hamiltons were so close, so united as a family. They were so old-fashioned in their views on family ties and family loyalties. Kyre would never listen to the most constructive criticisms on his family and seemed deaf to her hints that they imposed on him too much. It was a constant source of annoyance that they were content to shelter indefinitely in the shadow of his responsibility and to enjoy life at his expense. She did not appreciate his argument that his home would seem empty without his family about him. She was secretly contemptuous of his insistence that as the head of the family he had certain obligations and duties to fulfil.

Things would be different when they were married. There were ways and means of persuading Melanie and Philip that their presence was both an inconvenience and a proof of their lack of initiative in finding a home of their own. Old Aunt Dimity with her vague meanderings and all the evidence of advanced years would be much better off in a nursing home with proper care and attention. Uncle James was tolerable but he would have to be checked from wandering wherever he chose in the house and a hint should be sufficient to keep him in his own quarters. Kane and Cathryn must eventually marry — and then she and Kyre could enjoy the privacy and peace of this lovely old house. At the moment, there was little scope for entertaining on a large scale — and Honor enjoyed entertaining and would enjoy it even more when she was the mistress of Hamilton House.

She sensed the drawing together, the exclusion of her from their private grief and she was irritated. Randall had been dead for six months. Time might not erase the memory but it could certainly heal — and there was little point in continuing to mourn his death. She could not understand this silent insistence on a grief that it was sacrilege for anyone to mention.

In her opinion, Randall had been a reckless incorrigible rogue, loving fast cars, fast living and fast women . . . and he had carved his own destiny. She had never liked him and the dislike had been mutual. Randall had seemed to enjoy making Honor the butt of his satirical wit. She had thought him young and immature and selfish. She had been sorry when he had died so tragically but she had enjoyed her visits to Hamilton House so much more since fate had removed the possibility that Randall would be there on one of his brief, flying visits.

Honor was fond of Cathryn: it would be difficult to resist the appeal of the warm, good-natured girl who never bore malice and always considered the feelings of others in a way that her brother had never paused to do. Cathryn was good company, amusing and lively, easily pleased and swift to fall in with suggestions. Honor had enjoyed their day in town and she appreciated the fact that Cathryn had a natural good taste where clothes were concerned. One could always be sure of buying the right thing if it had Cathryn's approval — and she was always strictly honest in her comments.

She was an attractive, pleasant young woman and Honor admitted freely that the guardianship of his young cousins had not caused Kyre the heartburnings that she had anticipated. Randall had been a handful in the early days but Kyre had used tact and common sense in his dealings with the boy, and it was not his fault that maturity had done little for Randall but provide him with more freedom, more money and the right to make his own way to his tragic end.

She knew that his death had been a blow to Kyre and she had hoped to draw him to talk of his feelings. It was then that she had first met with that cold, courteous barrier that was always present now if she chanced to speak of Randall Hamilton . . .

They chatted desultorily, but Honor was conscious of a certain restraint in the atmosphere. She was sorry that she had hurt Cathryn and she tried to make amends — but the deeper she went the more she floundered and she knew that her subtle compliments and her frequent appeals to Cathryn were doing little to ease the effect of her tactless remarks about Randall.

Eventually she moved towards the door. 'It's time I changed for dinner,' she said lightly.

As soon as the door closed, Cathryn turned to her cousin. 'Oh, Kyre, she can be such an utter beast!'

He smiled gently — and his smile held a wealth of compassionate understanding. 'Isn't that a little strong?'

'Not strong enough for my feelings,' she said vehemently. 'She never liked

Randall — and even now she doesn't hesitate to show her dislike.'

'I don't think she meant to be unkind, darling,' he said quietly, loyal as ever to a friend.

She eyed him thoughtfully. 'Do you really mean to marry her, Kyre?'

He raised an eyebrow. 'Would it be such a blow?'

'Oh yes!' she said honestly. 'Honor isn't right for you, darling. She hasn't any warmth, any gentleness.' She gave a little shudder. 'She wouldn't fit in, Kyre.'

Kyre smiled. 'Then perhaps I'd better wait until you get married and have a home of your own,' he said lightly.

Cathryn stared at him blankly. 'Why, Kyre, you know I'd never leave this house even if I marry,' she said impetuously.

'The man you marry might not wish to settle in this house, surrounded by in-laws,' he reminded her.

'I shall choose my man more carefully,' she said firmly. She looked up at him. 'So you do mean to marry Honor?'

He gave a little shrug. 'Possibly. I thought you liked Honor. You have to admit that she would make a perfect mistress for this house — she has the right background, the right education, the right manner.'

'I can't forget that Randall never liked her — and he must have had his reasons,' she said firmly. 'He was never wrong about people, Kyre.'

He was surprised. It had not occurred to him that she tolerated Honor for his sake alone or that her brother's capricious likes and dislikes could so influence her. He had always believed that she liked and admired Honor Pattison — and certainly there had always been a friendly warmth between them.

It was true that Randall had never cared for Honor but he had believed that the boy's dislike stemmed from her cool, ill-concealed disapproval of his way of life. Also, Honor had little sense of humour and she had seldom appreciated his love of practical jokes or his lively, rather satirical wit. Randall had resented her disapproval, naturally enough, and deplored her lack of humour.

Cathryn went on quietly: 'Maybe she would make a good mistress for the house but she wouldn't make you a good wife, Kyre. She wants to dominate you, run your life according to her code. Why, she resents your work because it takes you away from her — and she resents all of us because you like to have us living with you.'

He chided her gently: 'Honor is our guest, darling. While she is under our roof let's agree not to criticise her. Honor has her faults — so have we all — but I've always found her to be a very good friend. In any case, I'm not even thinking of marriage at the moment . . . '

'Honor is, believe me,' she cut in swiftly, tartly.

He laughed. 'Women seldom think of

anything else.' His tone was teasing as he went on: 'Haven't you an ulterior motive for inviting Colin Hammond to dinner?'

Faint colour stole into her cheeks. 'Colin was Randall's closest friend.'

'And thus a candidate for your friendship?'

'I do like him,' she admitted. 'But there isn't anything silly about our friendship.'

'You're just good friends?' he suggested with a twinkle in his eyes.

She wrinkled her nose. 'Such a hackneyed phrase, darling.' She glanced at her neat wrist watch. 'Oh well, I suppose I'd better dress, too. I do hate having guests, Kyre. It's so much nicer when we're alone and can be as informal as we like.'

'Yes, I'm afraid we all have a natural laziness in that direction,' he said lightly. 'It's good for us to have people to stay occasionally — keeps us on our toes.'

When Cathryn had gone, moving with her lithe, attractive grace, he went to the fireplace and threw on some fresh logs. There was time for him to enjoy a last pipe before changing and he settled himself comfortably in his chair and reached for his pipe and pouch.

He agreed with Cathryn that it was a bore to change for dinner, but Honor made it obvious that she expected the meal to be afforded all the gracious dignity and formality of past days. In that respect, if no other, she had the alliance and support of old Jeffries and Mrs. Nunhead. They had been with the family for so many years that they enjoyed a certain freedom of speech and did not hesitate to express their disapproval of meals on a tray by the fire, of dining in the same clothes that they had worn all day, of informality and easy-going habits that they had slipped into throughout the years. They were openly delighted when friends came to stay: when the family were enjoying their privacy and solitude it was frequently pointed out that they should entertain more often; time enough to laze quietly in the evenings when they were old!

The Hamiltons were not an unsociable family: they enjoyed entertaining and being entertained as much as any of their friends; but they loved their home and each other and were content in each other's company; they could never be bored while they had music and books and conversation — and there were enough of them to provide a variety of subjects for conversation . . .

2

Kyre relaxed and drew on his pipe. His thoughts turned to Randall as they so frequently did when he was alone. He had been fond of the young man and had known that his love of fast cars and his outrageous flirtations were no more than the follies of youth. Randall had been sensible, sensitive and intelligent, gentle-natured and warm-hearted — and there had not been an ounce of vice in his make-up. His death had been a bitter pill to swallow — and it had been little comfort that he had obviously been on his way to visit his family at Hamilton House when the accident occurred. It had been three months since his previous visit and all had been wondering when they would see him again. He had been the restless member of the family, another James Hamilton, reluctant to settle down too early, wanting to enjoy all that life in town could offer yet inevitably returning to his home every few months, drawn by the love and the welcome that he was always confident of knowing on his return. They had known little of that town life for his comments were always light-hearted, gay, inconsequential, his conversation full of easy references to famous names, to theatres and clubs and parties, to friends he had made at Oxford, to 'fascinating types' he had met in London, telling his family a great deal that was unnecessary and little that was more to the point. But Kyre had not felt the need for anxiety. Randall had been sane and level-headed and it seemed unlikely that he would get involved in any scrapes that he could not extricate himself from with ease.

The Hamiltons had always been a clannish family. They were liked and respected by their neighbours and their opinions still carried weight, although their way of life might annoy some of the newcomers to the district who felt that it was an anachronism in this modern age.

Kyre, his twin brother Kane and their sister Melanie had been born in the old family house. Their mother had died when the twins were seven and Melanie eighteen months old. Kyre had stepped into his father's shoes as the head of the family on his death ten years before.

Melanie had been married for seven years but she continued to live at Hamilton House with her husband and two children. Uncle James had been a rolling stone for years before returning to England, still a bachelor, to spend the rest of his life at Hamilton House. His only sister, Dimity, had never married and never left the house in which she had been born. Their brother Martin had married an actress of some repute who had only interrupted her career to have her two children, Randall and Cathryn: both Martin and his lovely wife had died in an air crash when Randall was thirteen and Cathryn ten years old. Kyre had automatically taken over the guardianship of the two children and had always been more brother than cousin to both.

They were a united, affectionate family. They did not interfere in each other's lives. Kyre had converted a wing into a self-contained unit for Melanie and her family: Uncle James and Aunt Dimity had their own suite of rooms on the first floor; Kyre, Kane and Cathryn had their own privacy of bedrooms and sitting-rooms. There was ample room to absorb Cathryn's husband and possible children when she eventually married, another wing that remained to be converted when Kane made up his mind to marry and raise a family — and, Kyre, thought now with wry amusement as he mused over his pipe, thinking of these things, Honor would have to fit in where and as best she could if they married!

It was his affection and loyalty for his family that gave him pause whenever he debated this question of marriage. He fully realised that few women would want to share husband and home with his family — and he did not expect Honor to be an exception.

They had been friends for many years. She attracted him physically: mentally, they were fairly well attuned; they had a great deal in common, many mutual interests and mutual friends — and she was the obvious choice of a wife for him. Background, breeding, social position, intelligence and poise, beauty and a charming personality were among her many assets — but Kyre could not visualise her as a member of the Hamilton family . . .

As a guest, she got on very well with them all; as his wife and the mistress of the house, she would seek to instigate changes. He knew that only too well.

She would not always be patient with Aunty Dimity's vague sweetness and shy timidity or always be courteously interested when Uncle James embarked on the saga of his travels and adventures. While she professed to adore children, she was frankly bored after a few minutes in their company and it was doubtful that she would continue to be amused by the youthful, mischievous escapades of Melanie's infants when they touched her life more closely. She and Cathryn were on good terms, but would they continue to be friends if they lived under the same roof and Honor was tactless enough to show her disapproval too plainly or attempt to advise the younger woman on the way she should run her life.

Kyre pulled thoughtfully on his pipe. He would need to be very much in love with any woman before he married — and, for some obscure reason, that depth of affection was lacking where Honor was concerned. Perhaps they had known each other too long and too well. In all his thirty-five years, he had never been in love — and believed that he was incapable of loving any woman as a man should love the woman that he married.

He laid aside his pipe and rose reluctantly to his feet. He moved to the tall window and drew aside the heavy, richly-coloured curtains. It was a cold, rough, unfriendly night, the darkness coming quickly now that the year was rapidly approaching its end. It had been such a night when Randall was killed — wet, windy and dark — and Kyre would dearly love to know what had caused the small, ultra-modern sports car to spin off the road and crash into the cluster of tall trees at the foot of the hill.

He stood for a moment, looking towards the village and the bright pinpoints of light that indicated the small, homely cottages and farmhouses.

Then he frowned and leaned forward to peer into the gloom. Someone was laboriously making his way towards the house, body bent against the wind and rain. It was too dark to recognise the caller. Kyre could not even be sure if it were a man or woman. It was an odd time for anyone to call and few of his friends would choose to walk through the cold, wet evening when it was almost too dark to see one's way.

He hurried from the room and into the hall. Opening the heavy main door, he narrowed his eyes to ascertain the identity of the slowly approaching figure.

Sara's heart began to hammer more wildly as that blaze of light fell across her path. It seemed more of a threat than a welcome to the girl who was weary, damp, aching in every bone, hungry and thirsty — and dreading the meeting with the man she sought. She looked at the tall, casually-dressed man who hesitated on the threshold of the house, framed in the doorway by the light behind him, his face in shadow.

Kyre ran down the stone steps and into the rain. He reached Sara and took her arm. 'Only a few steps more,' he said encouragingly, sensing her distressed condition.

She knew an instinctive gratitude for his supporting arm, allowed her body to relax against him for a brief moment.

Then she stiffened and drew herself up with quiet dignity,

'I can manage, thank you.'

Kyre was puzzled by the hostility of her tone. He led the way into the house and hastily closed the door against the cold night. Then he smiled at the girl, so slight, so obvious in her condition, so weary in body and spirit. Had she lost her way in this foul weather and in the darkness of the winter night? Had she been defeated by the wind and rain and turned in at the first gate on her way? She was certainly in no condition to be battling with the elements, for one swift glance had assured him that the birth of her expected child could not be far distant.

Whatever the answer to his silent questions, there was nothing to be gained by standing in the hall and he threw open the door of his study.

'Come by the fire,' he said kindly.

Sara walked into the room, looking about her with a strange expression in her eyes. There was something of hostility, something of contempt, something of passionate anger. She was unmoved by his kindness and the gentle touch of his hand on her arm as he guided her to a chair. She sat down without relaxing her taut body.

Kyre looked down at her thoughtfully. Then he turned and pressed the bell that was set in the wall beside the fire-place. Whatever her business with him might be, hot coffee seemed an excellent idea — and it would help to ease the strange hostility of the atmosphere.

Sara watched him coldly. She guessed that this man must be one of the twins — he bore the unmistakable stamp of a Hamilton. She noted the arrogance of his features, the proud bearing, the hint of sensuality about his mouth and the inscrutable darkness of his eyes.

'Which one are you?' she asked abruptly.

Kyre could not mistake the defiant hostility of her tone this time. He turned to look at her. 'I'm Kyre

Hamilton,' he said quietly.

'So you are Kyre? The head of the house.' Her lip curled slightly.

It was an unmistakable jibe but Kyre merely smiled, determined not to be offended by anything she might say, any expression, however offensive, in her eyes, while she was so weary and her presence at Hamilton House was yet to be explained.

'Take off your coat,' he suggested, kicking the logs into a better position. 'It looks wet and you might catch cold.'

She drew the coat more closely about her slight, misshapen body. Kyre did not know whether to be annoyed or touched by that oddly defiant, ultra-sensitive gesture.

He smiled. 'That doesn't conceal anything, my dear,' he said gently. 'And I really don't think you should sit about in that damp coat.'

Colour surged into her pale cheeks but she made no move to remove the offending coat. Kyre would have insisted, gently but firmly, but the door opened at that moment and Jeffries came into the room. Kyre ordered the coffee, instilling enough urgency into his voice to ensure its swift arrival. When the door closed behind the elderly butler, Kyre turned back to his unexpected, mysterious guest.

'You look as though you've been walking for some time in the rain,' he said, glancing briefly at her mud-splashed legs and soaked shoes. 'I'm sure you'll appreciate some coffee.'

'I've walked from the station,' she said wearily. 'A fool of a porter told me that it was only a few minutes walk to this house. That was an understatement, of course — it must be all of three miles.'

'Quite an understatement,' he agreed, smiling. He was astonished that she had even walked so far in her condition and in such bad weather — even more surprised to realise that she had come to his house by design and not by accident. She was a complete stranger to him and her presence was an enigma. 'I'm sorry that you've had such a poor welcome,' he said tentatively.

Sara shrugged. 'I didn't expect anything else.'

Kyre was at a loss. It was an unusual state of affairs for him. He stood by the fire, staring into its bright flames, trying to fathom who or what she was and what she wanted with him or his family. He was thankful when Mrs. Nunhead bustled into the room with the tray and he moved swiftly to relieve her of the burden. She glanced curiously at Sara and then looked at him with a question in her eyes. He gave a faint shrug. He had known that Jeffries would hasten to the kitchen to tell of the stranger in their midst.

He waited until his housekeeper had left the room. Then he poured the steaming, fragrant coffee and placed her cup on a low table close to her hand. Questions were trembling on his lips but he checked them . . . better to let her drink her coffee and relax in the friendly warmth of the room. She must

35

eventually mention the purpose of her visit.

Sara looked at the cup blankly and then she shook her head. 'I don't want coffee. I want to see Randall. Is he here?'

The question thrust itself into the sudden silence and seemed to hover in the air. Kyre was stunned and shaken by the unexpectedness of her request.

'Randall?' He found his voice at last. 'But . . . surely . . . are you sure you mean Randall Hamilton?'

'Yes, of course.' Her tone was sharp, impatient.

'You knew Randall?' He was playing for time: it was obvious that she had known the boy . . . perhaps even owed her present condition to him, he thought with a sudden pang. Randall had been young, careless, fun-loving but surely not the type to take his pleasures without a thought for the consequences.

'Much to my regret.' Her voice was heavy with bitterness. She did not notice his use of the past tense.

Kyre was very thoughtful. 'Then . . . do you mean that he was responsible . . . ' He broke off, reluctant to put his suspicion into words, reluctant to embarrass her.

'No need to be so delicate, Mr. Hamilton,' Sara told him tartly. 'Of course Randall is the father of my child. Would I be here if it were otherwise?'

'I . . . I suppose not,' Kyre said awkwardly. 'Look, I'm completely at sea, I'm afraid, Miss . . . '

'I'm Sara,' she said impatiently. 'Surely Randall has told you about me?'

Kyre shook his head. He was very grave as he said quietly: 'I'm afraid not.'

'But that's ridiculous!' she exploded. 'I know he was tired of me but some obligations can't be brushed aside as though they'd never existed! He must have spoken of me at some time.'

'I've never heard him mention your name,' Kyre said truthfully.

'I'm Sara,' she repeated angrily. 'Sara Hamilton — Randall's wife!'

Kyre sat down abruptly. 'His . . . his

wife!' The shocked exclamation was forced from him.

Her mouth twisted in a bitter, mocking smile. 'So he did mean to walk out and forget all about me. It was the obvious answer, of course. Randall never does think of anyone or anything but himself and his own pleasure. But he almost convinced me that he intended to make arrangements for me to live here . . . '

Kyre leaned forward. 'I'm sorry to seem so obtuse, but would you clarify things for me? You say that Randall married you — may I ask when? And, although it might sound odd, if you're quite sure that you married my cousin and not someone who was using his name?'

Sara stiffened. 'We were married in February,' she said coldly. 'It was perfectly legal and I have the necessary proof.' She paused, rummaged in her handbag and produced a marriage certificate which she proudly thrust into his hands. 'Is that more convincing than my word, Mr. Hamilton?'

Kyre stared down at the document. The facts were clear enough, indisputable enough. Randall had certainly married this young woman if she were the Sara Winston whose name appeared on the certificate — and she had no reason to lie to him. The thought that Randall might have seduced her and given her a child was more welcome to him than the realisation that his was the task of telling her that she was a widow — and he could not be blamed from shrinking from it.

'But . . . why didn't we know?' It was barely more than a murmur, spoken more to himself than to the girl.

She laughed — a short, bitter sound that hurt and startled him. 'I suppose that is the joke in this affair. Randall told me that he was coming here to tell his family that he was married, to make arrangements for us to live here until we found a house of our own. He said that he wanted his child to be born here like all the Hamiltons. I couldn't come with him at the time but I trusted him to come back. I believed his assurances . . . until the days passed without word from him of any kind.' She went on angrily: 'Now . . . may I see Randall? I haven't come chasing him for myself — but I don't see why an innocent child should suffer because his father lacks principles! Why should I struggle to bring up his child alone when I have no money and no family — and Randall has both?'

Carefully, with more care than it merited, Kyre folded her marriage certificate. 'Did you love him . . . very much?' he asked gently.

'I married him,' she returned coldly.

'I don't mean to be impertinent,' he said quickly, fearing that his words had probed a naked wound. 'Sara . . . I must call you that . . . Sara, I wish I could welcome you to this house in happier circumstances,' Kyre said awkwardly, knowing that his words were stilted, dreading her reaction to the news that he must break, wishing that he could find the right words, the easy words.

She said stiffly: 'Oh, I haven't come to stay. I shall have this wretched infant and then go back to my own life. The child is Randall's concern once it's born.' Her tone was brittle, unnaturally harsh.

'Please . . . ' He spoke firmly, urgently. 'I have some bad news for you . . . news that isn't easy to break . . . '

'Randall doesn't want me or his child. Well, that isn't news! I've known it for months. I'm not a fool — and I haven't heard or seen anything of Randall in six months. The facts are obvious, aren't they? Anyway, I'm not interested in picking up old threads, if you must have the truth.'

He studied her for a long moment. Her voice was harsh, unemotional, cold — and he told himself that she could not be blamed for her bitterness. For six months she had believed herself to be a deserted wife with an ordeal to face alone. It was natural that she should feel that she hated and distrusted a man she had married with high hopes such a short time before his supposed desertion. He thought that she must have been very much in love with Randall . . . he wondered how and where the couple had met, why Randall had never spoken of this girl on that last visit to his home before his death, during that last Christmas that they had all spent together. Had theirs been a swift and sudden affair, a brightly burning flame of love ignited in a moment by a word, a glance, a gesture? Or had Randall known this strange young woman for a long time before persuading her into marriage? And why so much secrecy? Why had they married without a word to anyone, so quietly and discreetly, at a registry office?

He heard himself asking, almost abruptly: 'Why have you waited so long before trying to find out what had happened to Randall?'

She shrugged. 'I told you . . . I knew he was tired of me. There'd been quarrels. I can't understand why he should spout a stream of lies about coming here if he didn't mean to tell you about me and certainly didn't mean to come back for me. But I never could understand Randall. At times he could be so sweet, so lovable — and at others . . . ' She broke off and the ugliness of loathing touched her grey eyes. Kyre was briefly shocked by that expression. After a brief pause, she went on: 'I don't really know why I've left it so long. I suppose I was proud and thought I could manage without him . . . but there isn't any money coming in when you're expecting a baby and can't work — and there isn't any place for a child in my profession.'

'Your profession?' Kyre asked swiftly.

'I'm an actress.'

'Oh, I see.' Kyre's thoughts winged to Randall's mother who had also been an actress: the boy had always been interested in the theatre and had enjoyed meeting those people who had known his mother when she was a clever and popular actress; many of his friends had been theatrical types and no doubt he had met Sara Winston through a mutual friend. He dragged his thoughts back to the present. He could not continue to postpone the moment when he must tell her that her husband was dead.

3

'Why don't you send for Randall?' Sara asked impatiently. 'He won't be pleased to see me but it's about time he faced up to his responsibilities.'

'My dear, I am in a very difficult position,' he said quietly. 'You see . . . Randall isn't here.' It was lame and he knew it — but one could not simply blurt out the tragic truth without preliminary.

'Not here!' Sara caught her breath. The ordeal of her long journey had been a waste of time, after all! She had not expected to find Randall away from Hamilton House. During the past months she had looked for him in the restaurants and clubs that had been his usual haunts and when it was obvious that he was not in London she had assumed that he preferred to remain in the country for reasons of his own. She has hesitated to approach any of his friends because she had been too proud to admit that her husband had walked out. In answer to any enquiries, she had always said that Randall was in Kent on family business. She did not know if the enquirers were satisfied but her tone and bearing had been sufficient to ward off further questions. She looked steadily at Kyre Hamilton. 'Do you mean that he's with another woman?' she asked bluntly.

Kyre shook his head. 'No . . . I wish that were the answer, Sara.' He leaned forward and took possession of her hands. She was surprised and wary but she did not draw her hands away from that gentle clasp. He said quietly, compassionately: 'Randall was killed . . . on his way here in May. His car . . . we don't really know what happened.'

Sara stiffened. Horror and incredulity leaped to her eyes and she was conscious once more of pain that seemed to rip through her body.

'No,' she said tautly. 'No . . . you're lying — lying to shield him!'

'Would I lie about such a thing?' he asked with some heat.

Sara searched his face, recognised the honesty and the integrity in his dark eyes, shrank from the compassion and tenderness that were so evident.

'So he's dead?'

There was a curious flatness in her tone, a lack of feeling, even indifference. Kyre was thankful that there were no tears, no hysterics, no fainting girl on his hands — but he realised that this numbness, this shocked, cold acceptance was unnatural and dangerous.

Her small body was tensed and the blood abruptly receded from her face, leaving her with a deathly pallor. She had not known that having a baby would mean so much agony and she knew that she had been foolish to make the long journey into Kent with the knowledge that her child was soon to be born. But, for all Randall's faults, this child had been fathered by him and not even his supposed desertion had wiped out her solemn promise that the new member of the Hamilton family should be born in the old house that had belonged to them for generations.

Kyre realised instantly that she was in pain. Gently he eased her back into the chair and brushed the damp, fine hair from her small face. She bit her lip so fiercely that the taste of blood was in her mouth, determined that no pain, however hard to bear, would make her cry out. Kyre rang the bell urgently, moved swiftly to the decanters and poured brandy into a glass. He forced the liquid between her reluctant lips.

'There's nothing to worry about,' he said calmly. 'You're in good hands now, Sara. Your baby . . . it's on its way, isn't it?'

She nodded dumbly, the momentary panic subsiding as his calmness and quiet reassurance made the required effect.

Jeffries came into the room and took in the situation at a glance. 'I'll get

Mrs. Nunhead,' he stammered and hurried away. Within a very few minutes, the buxom neatly-dressed housekeeper came into the room.

'Whatever is it, Mr. Kyre?' she asked anxiously, glancing at the girl and noting the white face and the clenched hands.

'I want Mr. Randall's old room prepared immediately — hot bottles in the bed the fire going and Marsden sent for . . . tell him it's urgent,' he said without wasting time with explanations.

'Yes, of course, Mr. Kyre.' She bustled out and Kyre thanked heaven for reliable staff.

Sara struggled to sit up. 'I can't stay here,' she said wearily.

'My dear girl, you're in no condition to leave this house,' he said quietly. 'Anyway, don't you want your child to be born here . . . it's a Hamilton, after all.'

'Yes . . . that's why I came,' she admitted flatly.

His gaze was stern as it rested on

Sara. 'You knew, didn't you, Sara? You knew that your child would be born today?' She did not attempt to deny his accusation. He went on: 'But you travelled down here alone. That wasn't very sensible of you, my dear.'

She said hopelessly: 'I promised Randall . . .'

'You left it rather late,' he said grimly. Then he added quietly: 'But never mind that now. Bed is the best place for you and Marsden should be here within the hour. He's been our family doctor for years and he'll look after you, Sara.' He smiled gently. 'Do you think you can manage the stairs?'

'Of course!' she said proudly. She rose awkwardly to her feet and prayed that the pain would not return until she was safely in bed.

'Good girl!'

'This is all rather inconvenient for you, I'm afraid,' she said stiffly.

'Oh, we'll take it in our stride, I expect,' he said lightly.

Cathryn came into the room at that

moment, dressed for the evening, a light reprimand on her lips for his tardiness. The words trailed away as she realised that he was not alone — and she looked with obvious curiosity at the girl whose hands gripped the back of a chair with fierce intensity.

'I'm sorry, Kyre. I didn't know you were busy,' she said immediately.

As she turned to go, he said quickly: 'Don't go, Cathryn. I'll just take Sara to her room and then I'll be back.'

He looked at Sara and reluctantly she released her grip on the supporting chair and moved towards the door, too weary and too concerned with warding off pain to give more than an indifferent glance in Cathryn's direction. She scarcely registered the girl's name in that moment or realised that she was meeting her sister-in-law for the first time.

Cathryn said impulsively: 'Can I help?'

Kyre shook his head. 'Just wait here for me, darling.' There was a warning in his eyes and in the tone of his voice — and Cathryn stood aside and watched him and the stranger as they went from the room.

Intent on her preparations for the evening, Cathryn had known nothing of the bustling activity of Mrs. Nunhead and the young girl who helped her in the house as they carried out Kyre's instruction. Now, she thoughtfully helped herself to a cigarette, wondering about the girl and impatient for Kyre's return . . .

It was with a tiny pang that Kyre opened the door of the room that had been Randall's for so many years. His well-thumbed books still rested on their shelves, the skilful sketch of Cathryn that he had executed one summer afternoon still hung above the open fireplace, his brushes still lay on the dressing-table and, despite Mrs. Nunhead's regular attentions, there was the familiar stamp of Randall's untidy personality in the atmosphere of the room.

Mrs. Nunhead turned. 'I've borrowed one of Miss Cathryn's nightdresses for the young lady, Mr. Kyre . . . and I've sent Emily down for some hot soup.'

'This is Mrs. Hamilton . . . Mrs. Randall Hamilton,' Kyre said and his tone brooked no display of surprise, no argument, no question. He smiled at Sara. 'This is Mrs. Nunhead, Sara. She has been with us for years and practically brought us up in the right ways. She'll get you anything you want and stay with you until the doctor arrives. I shall come up to see you later, of course.'

Sara looked about the room with indifference born of a single-minded desire to lie down in the bed and ease her aching body and fight the threatening pain.

'Of course I'll look after Mrs. Hamilton. Now you run along and change for dinner, Mr. Kyre.' Like the good soul that she was, she showed no surprise and only concerned herself with the needs of the moment — and she recognised immediately that Sara's first need was rest and expert medical care.

Kyre smiled. So had Mrs. Nunhead spoken to him when he was a schoolboy who loved to watch her at work in the kitchen and she found him too much under her feet. He knew that he could safely leave Sara in those kindly, capable hands — and he was grateful for the calm acceptance of the introduction and the lack of curiosity.

He moved towards the door and laid a hand briefly on Sara's thin shoulder in passing. She looked up at him uncertainly and he knew that she was still very much on the defensive. The poor girl had been through rough waters and she was not yet in safe harbour — but he was thankful that she had come to Hamilton House in time to hand herself into their care and to have her child beneath its welcoming roof.

'My case,' she said slowly. 'I left it at the station. I didn't know if . . . ' Her voice trailed off.

'Oh, that's all right. I'll send someone to collect it,' he told her lightly.

Mrs. Nunhead hurried to help Sara remove her coat and she tutted disapprovingly over its wet condition. Kyre went from the room, faced with the task of telling the family about Randall's widow and knowing that he would be plied with a great many questions to which he did not know the answers.

'He's . . . very kind,' Sara said stiffly.

'Mr. Kyre? Oh, he's a grand young man — and kindness is as natural as breathing to him,' Mrs. Nunhead said briskly. 'Now, my dear, slip out of those clothes and into bed. It's the best place for you — you're not looking at all well.'

Sara smiled faintly. She was grateful for the helpful ministrations and she could not suppress a sigh of relief as the welcoming bed took the slight weight of her body and offered ease for its weariness.

Mrs. Nunhead bustled about the room, putting away Sara's clothes, bringing magazines, replenishing the fire which was already giving a pleasant warmth to the room. She glanced at Sara as she lay in the bed with closed eyes and clenched hands and there was an appraising look in her eyes. The unexpected guest had been introduced as Mr. Randall's widow — and certainly she wore a wedding ring. But the old lady had her private doubts about her right to that ring. It was not her place to ask questions or to betray her incredulity — but Mr. Randall would never have married anyone without telling his family and friends and planning a big celebration. The girl had her obvious reasons for claiming to be his widow — but Mr. Kyre would not be easily deceived. He would not turn away anyone who sought his help and kindness — certainly not a girl in that condition . . . but he would waste no time in checking whether or not she had any right to Mr. Randall's name!

Cathryn turned eagerly as Kyre entered. 'Darling, who is she?' she demanded. 'I'm eaten alive with curiosity! Don't tell me your past is catching up with you!'

Her flippancy jarred on him for his thoughts had been sombre. 'Don't joke, Cathryn! This isn't a joking matter!'

She was startled by his sharp tone. 'I'm sorry, Kyre,' she said meekly.

He smiled at that crestfallen face. 'So am I. I didn't mean to snap — but I haven't particularly enjoyed the last half-hour.' He sat down wearily. 'Pour me a drink, darling — and then I'll assuage your curiosity.'

She obeyed him. Kyre sipped his drink and stared into the fire. Cathryn resumed the chair she had left on his entry and perched on the edge in her impatient eagerness. 'Well?' she prompted.

'I've a surprise for you,' he said quietly. 'That girl is your sister-in-law.'

She stared at him without comprehension. 'My . . . sister-in-law?'

'Randall's widow,' he clarified soberly.

'Randall? You mean . . . he married

that girl? I don't believe it! Kyre, you don't believe it, surely? It can't be true!'

'I've seen the marriage certificate.'

'And it is true? Randall was married?'

Kyre nodded. 'In February. I suppose he was on his way to tell us about his marriage when . . . '

'But Randall wouldn't do a thing like that,' she objected, breaking into his words. 'Why, he told me everything!'

'And you never knew him to mention a Sara Winston?'

'Sara Winston . . . ? Is that her name? Sara . . . no, I've never heard it,' she said flatly.

'Are you quite sure?'

She wrinkled her forehead. 'Randall knew so many girls — and each one was *the* girl . . . until he met someone else. I didn't think he'd ever settle down with one woman. He did say something about a girl he met at a party just before Christmas . . . he seemed smitten but he said she was already attached and there wasn't any hope for him. I didn't take much notice, I'm afraid. Randall was so impetuous about women.' She looked steadily at her cousin. 'Do you think this might be that girl?'

He shrugged. 'I don't know. But I do believe that she married Randall in February.'

'Then why on earth didn't we know about it?'

'I suppose they had their reasons for secrecy.'

'Assuming that they did, why hasn't she bothered to get in touch with us until now?' Cathryn demanded suspiciously.

'Because she didn't know that Randall was dead . . . she thought he had left her,' he explained.

'Oh, Kyre . . . that's awfully weak! No one would simply accept their husband's desertion without doing *something* about it! And, well, she's going to have a baby, isn't she? Even more reason to hare after one's husband at the earliest moment!'

'So one would think,' he agreed. 'But she seems to have plenty of pride.'

'Maybe it isn't Randall's child,' Cathryn said quickly, sceptically. 'Perhaps he left her on the spot when he found out — she could so easily pretend that nothing was wrong and persuade him to marry her. Now that he's dead perhaps she hopes we'll accept her child as Randall's without question.'

'You're leaping to conclusions, darling. We shall never know why Randall was coming here . . . but I believe Sara's story that he meant to tell us about his marriage and arrange for them both to live here. I don't think she would lie. She certainly didn't know about his death, Cathryn — and if it wasn't Randall's child she wouldn't have risked coming here to be exposed by him.'

'And she really married him?' Cathryn could not grasp the simple fact . . . she had to put the question once more.

'Yes . . . at Caxton Hall . . . February 14th, I think.'

'Just nine months ago,' she mused

thoughtfully. 'When does she expect her baby?'

'At any moment, I imagine,' he said grimly. 'I don't know when she expected it, but it will probably arrive today. I've sent for Marsden, anyway.'

'So we have to assume that it's Randall's child?'

'We have no reason to doubt it,' he reminded her quietly. He leaned forward abruptly. 'Cathryn, be kind — try to imagine how you would feel in similar circumstances. She has had a rough time — and she needs all the help and kindness that we can give.'

She was silent, thinking of the brother she had loved and mourned, puzzled by the secrecy of his marriage, suspicious of the girl who had arrived at Hamilton House to claim that she was his widow. It seemed incredible that Randall would have married anyone without breaking the news to his family . . . and he had declared often enough that he was not cut out for marriage, that he liked to love them and leave them when the gilt wore off the gingerbread. She had been granted little opportunity to study the girl who claimed to be his widow, but that brief inspection did not convince Cathryn that she was the type to captivate her brother so much that he had married her.

At last she said proudly: 'Do you really think I could be unkind to someone that Randall loved? He must have been in love because he wasn't very keen on tying himself up for life with anyone. I can scarcely believe it yet but I wouldn't dream of making her feel unwelcome. What did you think of her, Kyre? Did you like her?'

'I'm sorry for her,' he said honestly. 'I've scarcely had time to find out if I like her, Cathryn. She's ill and tired and shocked — scarcely the right circumstances for impressions, good or bad. She's very much on the defensive, of course. She came here believing that Randall had deserted her and determined to make him face up to his responsibilities. She was angry and proud and resentful — quite naturally. I don't know how she feels now . . . probably too concerned with her coming infant to feel Randall's death very deeply at the moment. It will come home to her more forcibly after her child is born, I expect.'

Cathryn offered him a cigarette and then bent her dark head over the flame of the table lighter. 'As you say, one can scarcely judge her at the moment . . . but she doesn't seem the type that Randall used to find attractive.'

He shrugged. 'I haven't seen her when she isn't tired and obviously pregnant,' he said. 'And neither have you, darling.'

She leaned back in her chair and blew smoke rings, her eyes inscrutable. 'It will be rather nice to have a baby in the house again,' she said idly. 'Is she really in labour now, Kyre?'

'How should I know? I'm not an expert in these matters,' he said impatiently. He glanced at his watch. 'Marsden should be here soon . . . you can ask him after he's seen Sara.'

'Poor Kyre,' she said unexpectedly. 'You certainly do get the burdens, don't you? You didn't bargain for this extra responsibility . . . Randall's widow and infant.'

'The house is big enough,' he replied briefly.

'I suppose she will stay here?'

'I don't know. It isn't likely that she'll leave a small baby to the care of people who are, after all, strangers in her eyes.'

'You can't prevent her from leaving and taking the baby with her,' Cathryn pointed out.

'I don't think that is her intention,' he said slowly. 'She says that she is an actress — and that there isn't any place for a child in her profession. That's true enough. Your mother realised the difficulties of combining a career with domesticity.'

'Then she *is* the girl that Randall mentioned! He told me she was an actress,' Cathryn exclaimed. 'She'll want to get back to the theatre as soon as possible, Kyre — and I expect she will leave her baby here. That's probably her sole reason for coming here . . . because she doesn't want the baby!'

'From all accounts, she hasn't had much reason to welcome it,' Kyre said. 'But she'll change her mind when it's born.'

She looked at him thoughtfully. 'You don't seem at all perturbed by the thought of providing for her and the child, Kyre.'

He smiled. 'Why should I? Two more mouths to feed won't make much difference — and Carol can look after the baby. Vanessa is almost too old for a nurse now, anyway — and it will give Carol something to do.'

The door opened quietly and Jeffries came in, old, bent, white-haired but still the dignified, responsible butler.

'Shall I serve dinner, sir?' There was a faint note of reproof in his voice.

Kyre rose to his feet. 'Lord, it's late! Give me ten minutes to change, will you, Jeffries?'

Cathryn rose, too. 'Will you tell the family at dinner?'

He grimaced. 'I shall have to, won't I?' He grinned suddenly at his cousin. 'Sometimes I wish Kane had been as impatient to be born as he is with life — then these unenviable tasks would be his lot and not mine!'

4

Cathryn accompanied him into the hall and then left him to enter the large, comfortable sitting-room where they were wont to gather in the evenings.

Only the children were missing from the family group. Uncle James was standing on the hearth with his hands held out to the bright flames. Having travelled extensively in the warmer countries for most of his life, he found the English climate a severe trial. He was a tall, distinguished man in his seventies, his dark hair streaked with white at the temples, the Hamilton features a little craggy with age. His sister Dimity was knitting placidly, a small, frail-looking woman with the delicate peaches and cream complexion of a young girl and silvery hair that framed a sweet and gentle face.

Kane was talking to Philip, a

big-boned young American who had come on a visit to England, fallen in love with Melanie Hamilton and remained to marry her and spend his days happily at the big house. Kane was very like his twin, tall, attractive, lithe, but his mouth had more sensuality than sensitivity, and there was more than a hint of arrogance in the moulding of his features. He looked after the estate while Kyre wrote his books and supplemented the family income, which had suffered from death duties and taxation throughout the years. Kane managed the estate capably and loved the land but his impatience and hot temper and undeniable arrogance did not make him very popular with the men he employed.

Melanie and Honor Pattison were seated together on a long couch. Melanie talked eagerly of her two small children while Honor assumed an expression of interest and scarcely concealed her boredom with the subject. Melanie was tall and her dark hair was braided neatly about her proud head. Marriage and motherhood had smoothed the pride and arrogance from her features, mellowed the swift temper and impatience that were Hamilton characteristics and sweetened the nature that had once been imperious and wilful and somewhat selfish. She adored her good-natured husband and had proved an excellent mother to their two children: the girl who had enjoyed the social round so much and flaunted her conquests had matured into a woman content with home and family and domestic interests.

Uncle James turned with an impatient frown as Cathryn entered. 'Where is that young man?' he demanded. 'Jeffries is waiting to announce dinner — and everyone is hungry!'

Cathryn rumpled his hair teasingly, raising herself on her toes. 'Old crosspatch! Kyre won't be many minutes.'

'No idea of time . . . these young people,' the old man grumbled.

Aunt Dimity looked up from her knitting, anxiety touching her faded blue eyes. 'Kyre isn't ill? I heard Jeffries telephoning Marsden a little while ago.'

Cathryn bent to kiss the smooth, delicate cheek. 'No, of course not,' she said reassuringly. 'That sleeve should be long enough for Vanessa, don't you think, Aunt Dimity? Did you choose the wool? I do like that colour.'

Melanie called: 'What is all the commotion, Cathryn? Mrs. Nunhead has been in and out of Randall's room and Emily has been scurrying up and down the stairs for the past half hour.'

'Oh, Kyre will explain,' she said carelessly. 'How are the children? Have they been good?'

'Not too bad . . . they're in bed and asleep, I hope,' she returned absently. 'Philip, get me another drink, please.'

Philip took her glass and obediently crossed to the decanters. Over his shoulder he said easily: 'Did you enjoy your day in town, Cathryn?'

'Lovely, thanks. I couldn't match

those glasses for you, I'm afraid — but I didn't have time for a thorough search.'

'Never mind . . . I'll probably get to London before Christmas,' he said carelessly. 'Can I give you a drink?'

'No, thanks . . . I've just had one with Kyre.' She turned to Kane, who was studying her with a gleam of amusement in his dark eyes. 'Colin is coming down for a few days next week, Kane. I met him in town.'

'You'll never earn your living in the theatre,' he said slowly, mockingly. 'Something is up, my dear Cathryn. You're doing your best but we all know that there's a mysterious stranger in the house — and it's obvious that you're afraid of giving the game away. What's going on, Cathryn? Everyone is at sixes and sevens this evening.'

Kyre entered before Cathryn could reply. He scarcely had time to speak a general greeting before the dinner gong resounded.

Uncle James moved slowly towards the door, leaning heavily on his cane.

No one had ever learned the true story that had caused his lameness, for the old man's account of his adventures differed with every telling. 'About time,' he said fretfully. 'Regular meals and regular habits keep a man young ... I can't abide being messed about. You must have a word with the servants, Kyre, my boy.'

Aunt Dimity hastened to put away her knitting, dropped the ball of wool, found that she had mislaid the pattern, struggled to her feet and nearly fell as she realised that the wool was entangled in her old-fashioned, laced shoes. Cathryn hurried to her assistance. 'I'm so sorry ... silly of me ... thank you, dear. Oh, dear, I'm keeping everyone waiting ... ' She smiled a vague, sweet apology.

'There's plenty of time, Aunt Dimity.' Kyre stooped to pick up the missing knitting pattern and handed it to his aunt.

'I've been pumping Cathryn to find out what matter of urgency demands

Marsden's presence,' Kane said lightly. 'Is it the girl in Randall's old room?'

Kyre looked at him swiftly. 'You don't miss much, Kane.'

He laughed. 'I tackled Emily. She was taking a tray into the room — and absolutely bursting with news.'

'What did she tell you?'

'Not very much. She obviously didn't know much and was dying to know more.'

'I'll explain while we eat,' Kyre said firmly and followed his uncle from the room. The others trailed after him, Honor with Melanie and Philip, Cathryn and Aunt Dimity, and Kane bringing up the rear.

Conversation was fairly light, touching on varied subjects, while the servants were in the room, but there was an undercurrent of impatient curiosity, encouraged by the unmistakable sounds of the doctor's arrival and Kyre's abrupt departure from the table to welcome him and to explain the reason for his presence. When he returned, the family plied him with eager questions.

He smiled faintly. 'One at a time, please!'

'The most pressing mystery is the identity of the young woman,' Kane drawled. 'It's obvious that Marsden has been called in to attend to her. Who the devil is she, Kyre?'

He pushed away his plate with its almost untouched food. 'Randall was married in February, very quietly — his widow arrived here this evening. She's expecting his child — and she didn't know that Randall was dead.' He spoke bluntly, almost wearily.

Cries of astonishment and doubt greeted his words. Cathryn sat silent, toying with her food: Honor turned to Kyre with amused scepticism in her eyes; Melanie and Philip began a heated discussion on the rights of a *posthumous* child that had nothing to do with the bombshell that Kyre had exploded in their midst.

Uncle James said stoutly: 'Nonsense! Pack of lies! You should have sent her about her business, Kyre!'

Kane turned to Cathryn: 'The dark horse! A secret marriage . . . shades of romantic novellettes! One assumes that he had his reasons — *if* it's true!'

Honor said lightly, mockingly: 'Really, Kyre! I didn't think you could be taken in so easily!'

Aunt Dimity's gentle voice broke through the hubbub: 'Poor child . . . I hope you were kind to her, Kyre, my dear.'

Kyre smiled at his aunt. It was a singularly sweet and affectionate smile. 'I think so, Aunt Dimity. I hope you will visit her later . . . it would be rather nice for Sara to feel that someone in this family offers her a welcome.' He turned to his uncle. 'It isn't lies, Uncle James. I've seen the marriage certificate — and I would have believed her story without that evidence. Melanie — did you keep Vanessa's baby clothes? I don't know if Sara has anything for her child but it would be nice of you to make the offer — they'll be needed very soon, I believe.'

Taken aback, Melanie coloured slightly. 'Why . . . yes, I still have them, Kyre. I'll look them out.'

Kyre pushed back his chair. 'Now, if you'll excuse me, I must talk to Marsden.'

His exit was the signal for the hubbub to break out again as the family discussed the disturbing and rather dramatic arrival of Sara Hamilton. Aunt Dimity remained aloof from the conversation, her blue eyes thoughtful and a faint smile touching her mouth.

Melanie was the first to follow Kyre from the room. 'I suppose I'd better find these baby clothes and see if there's anything I can do.'

Gradually the others drifted into the sitting-room where they sat over the coffee-cups, discussing the matter until there was scarcely anything left to discuss . . .

Marsden, a grim and taciturn man, left Kyre in little doubt that Sara's child would be born that night. He admitted frankly that he was anxious . . . the mother was already near to exhaustion and she was built on slim lines. It would probably be a difficult and prolonged birth but he would do all he could in the circumstances. He remarked grimly that he should have been called in earlier — and Kyre reluctantly explained that Mrs. Hamilton had only arrived at the house early that evening. Marsden did not comment on the name: no doubt he had met with stranger circumstances during his years of general practice.

'How is she at the moment?' Kyre asked.

'Resting.'

'May I see her for a few minutes?'

Marsden shrugged. 'If you must.'

'You don't advise it?'

'Oh, it can't do any harm. Only a few minutes, mind,' he warned.

Kyre nodded and quietly entered the bedroom. Sara was lying on her side, her blonde hair streaming across the pillows, darkened with the dampness of perspiration. Her eyes were closed. Kyre drew a chair nearer to the bed and sat down. He touched her hand gently and, startled, she opened her eyes.

'How do you feel?'

'Terrified,' she said and her lips trembled.

He was touched and a little surprised by her honesty. 'Marsden will do everything he can,' he said quietly.

'I know . . . he explained,' she said, moistening her dry lips.

'It won't be long now,' he assured her, hoping it was the truth. 'You want to see your baby, don't you?'

'Not particularly. It doesn't mean anything but a lot of pain.'

He was vaguely shocked . . . but he remembered Melanie in the last hours before the birth of her children and wondered if all women experienced this lack of feeling for the baby that brought pain with its birth.

'You won't feel like that in the morning,' he said, smiling.

Her grey eyes met his coldly. 'Have

you ever had a baby?'

His smile broadened. 'No . . . but my sister has had two.'

'I wouldn't go through this twice for any man,' she said almost under her breath.

So had Melanie spoken when Hamilton was born — but she had been thrilled and happy and fearless when she learned that another baby was on the way. One day Sara would fall in love again, marry again and welcome the advent of another child — for time dulled the memory and the maternal instinct was strong in most women.

'I mustn't stay any longer now,' he said, rising. 'I shall see you again tomorrow — and then you can show me your baby.' Gently he brushed a damp tendril of hair from her face . . . the pallor of exhaustion, the lingering memory of recent pain in her eyes, the tense anticipation of that slight body, the harsh weariness in her voice — these things evoked a tenderness and a compassion in him for the suffering of others caused him an almost physical pain.

She did not reply. Engulfed in the onslaught of agony, she blindly groped for his hand and he clasped her fingers reassuringly, murmuring words that soothed and comforted although they had little coherence. Sweat beaded her forehead and her mouth was drawn with pain, but she made no sound and he admired her courage and fortitude. At last she relaxed and her fingers slipped from his hand.

'Thanks . . . ' It was scarcely more than a murmur. She lay back on the pillows, breathing hard, but a trace of a smile flickered about her lips. 'I'm afraid . . . you didn't expect . . . this kind of thing, Mr. Hamilton.'

'My name is Kyre,' he amended quietly. He went from the room and tackled Marsden: 'How much more of that will she have to take, Marsden? Surely there's something you can do to hurry things up?'

'She's managing very well by herself.'

There was a definite reproof in the tone of his voice. 'Nature doesn't like interference . . . and I don't like anxious fathers on the scene, Mr. Hamilton. You'll know soon enough when the baby is here . . . and then you can see your wife again. She'll be tired but feeling much better — and then you'll realise that your anxieties were groundless.' He gave a curt little nod, entered the room and closed the door firmly behind him.

Kyre stared at the closed door. So Marsden had assumed that Sara was *his* wife . . . an easy mistake for he had spoken of her as Mrs. Hamilton and certainly he must seem concerned enough to be the father of her baby. A grim little smile played about his lips. He had not enjoyed holding her hand while she suffered . . . he could not imagine what his feelings would be if she had indeed been his wife. He did not think that he could ever sanction any woman going through that ordeal to give *him* a child!

Slowly he descended the stairs and crossed the hall to his study. He could hear voices from the sitting-room and felt that he was not in the mood to face the family again at that particular moment.

He closed the study door with a tiny snap of finality. Honor rose from the armchair that faced the fire. 'There you are, Kyre. I thought, you would come in here.' She looked at him curiously. 'What's the matter? You look quite drained . . . I'll get you a drink.'

'Thanks.' He sat down and stared moodily into the fire. Her presence in the room irritated him unreasonably. He should not resent her easy familiarity, her impression of long intimacy, the feeling that she took for granted his wish to talk to her although he might avoid his family. There were times when she behaved as though they had been married for years, he thought irritably — and took the glass from her hand without a word.

Honor raised an eyebrow. Then she

sat down and took a cigarette from the box. 'Well . . . ? What's going on?'

'I imagine that must be obvious,' he said coldly.

'The baby hasn't arrived yet?'

'Not yet.' His tone was curt, discouraging.

'You seem quite upset about all this, Kyre,' she said with a little laugh. 'Women have babies every day of the week . . . there's really nothing to it, you know. One would almost think that you had a personal interest in Randall's widow.'

He was annoyed by her slighting dismissal of the ordeal that Sara was going through in that room above his head.

Honor went on smoothly: 'If she really is his widow, of course — and you seem to believe her story. Why has there been so much secrecy? Was it one of these hasty, compulsory affairs, do you think?'

'No, I don't think,' he retorted crisply. 'Randall was married in February — we are now almost into December. Why is it that women always put the wrong and the most distasteful construction on everything? Randall was of age — he needed no one's permission to marry and if he chose to be married quietly and without telling his family or his friends . . . then that was his affair. I don't intend to question Sara about the matter at the moment — or at any time, in fact. If she wants me to know she will tell me — if she knows herself!'

Honor pursed her lips and tossed her half-smoked cigarette into the fire, rising to her feet. 'You're obviously in no mood for my company, Kyre,' she said coolly.

He looked at her. 'I'm sorry, Honor,' he said, feeling bound to offer the apology she so obviously expected. 'But I would like to be alone for a while . . . if you don't mind?' He sighed his relief as the door closed and he was able to relax. Perhaps he had been a little hard on Honor — but it was amazing that she understood him so little after so many years. He stretched his long legs to the fire — and reached for his pipe . . .

Some time later, a light tap on the door brought him from his reverie. The door opened and Melanie came into the room. 'Am I disturbing you, Kyre?'

'No, not really.' He smiled at his sister. 'What is it?'

'I've looked out some baby clothes,' she said lightly. 'Vanessa had so many things that some of them have never been worn. Marsden is still upstairs . . . I suppose you don't know what's happening, Kyre?'

He shrugged. 'Apart from the fact that the baby should arrive tonight, I don't know anything. Marsden seems fairly confident that everything will be all right — but surely it's taking a long time?' There was a note of anxiety in his quiet voice.

'First babies always take their time,' she said easily. 'Don't you remember how it was with Hamilton?' She took the cigarette that he offered, bent her head over the flame of the table lighter and then perched easily on the arm of a chair, looking at him thoughtfully. 'It's a funny business, isn't it, Kyre? Randall being married, I mean . . . surely we would have known about it? *Someone* would have known . . . his friends, the witnesses at the wedding — and what happens now?'

'A lot of things have to be sorted out now,' Kyre said. 'Randall must have intended to tell us about his marriage — in his own good time. He didn't expect to die in such a way and at his age. One would think that some of his friends knew about it . . . but he had a great many friends that we don't know and no doubt they assumed that his family knew. After all, would you contact the family of a friend after her death and say: Look here, I don't know if you're aware of it but Sheila or Janet or Hilda was married and don't you think you should do something about her husband?'

Melanie smiled. 'No, of course not.'

'Exactly.'

'I get your point. So you had to explain about the accident? How did she take it?'

'Quite unemotionally,' he admitted. 'It must have been a shock but she didn't betray her feelings. She's an actress — did Cathryn tell you? I expect she knows how to keep her self-possession even in the circumstances.'

'Oh, we've pumped Cathryn dry,' she said, laughing. 'It's the solitary subject of conversation tonight, I'm afraid. We shall be awfully dull when all this excitement comes to an end.'

'I expect we shall,' he said drily.

She rose and stretched her tall, lithe body. 'Oh, well, I'd better get back to the others. You didn't mind me coming in for a few minutes?'

Kyre smiled. 'Of course not. Honor had spread the word that I'm in bad humour, has she?'

She coloured faintly. 'She did say that you seemed tired and a little irritable.'

'I am tired — but I'm not at all irritable,' he assured her. 'Perhaps

Honor's matter-of-fact attitude to it all jarred on me a little . . . I can't help feeling rather closely concerned in this business.'

Melanie lightly brushed his dark hair with her lips. 'You're such a sensitive old boy,' she said affectionately. 'I'm sure you suffered more than I did when my infants were born. I don't suppose there's anything to worry about, you know . . . Marsden may be a dour old stick but he does know his job — and he won't let Sara have too much pain . . . he was marvellous to me both times!'

'Yes, I know.' He patted her hand. 'Melanie, am I making too much of it all? Should I be eagerly churning it over with the family and regarding it as an exciting little titbit to enliven the dullness of our lives?'

Melanie laughed. 'I'm afraid we are viewing it in that light, Kyre. Not that our lives *are* dull, by any means — but it's a new subject for conversation, after all. You needn't feel guilty, darling. Someone has to feel a sense of responsibility for Randall's widow ... someone has to show a more personal concern or the poor girl would feel herself quite unwanted.' She moved towards the door. 'I'll give the things to Mrs. Nunhead, shall I? She and Emily and Carol are busily preparing the nursery ... it seems an age since Vanessa was young enough to need it!'

5

The house seemed very quiet after his sister had left him. Kyre mused over Melanie's words. She understood him very well and she always knew exactly the right thing to say in all circumstances. She was an intelligent and sensitive young woman and he thought now that if she were to take a liking to Sara Hamilton then the girl would be assured of a welcome from one member of the family at least.

He could not make up his mind if he welcomed her to his house. It had been a shock to learn that Randall was married without their knowledge — and there was something in the girl's attitude which puzzled him. It seemed more than ordinary resentment and bitterness at her husband's presumed desertion at a time when he was most needed. Her acceptance of his death, even allowing for her state of mind and the shock it must have been, had been strange — almost although she learned of the death of a man to whom she had been completely indifferent. Had she regretted her marriage so swiftly? Had Randall been unsatisfactory, difficult, disappointing as a husband? His good humour, his charm, his inbred courtesy, his *joie de vivre* had ensured him liking and popularity . . . even if, as she had claimed, Randall had quickly tired of the girl he had married it seemed out of character to believe that he could have behaved in a way calculated to earn his wife's loathing so quickly. Yet he had not mistaken that swift flash of contemptuous hatred in her eyes. Sara Hamilton had reason, real or imaginary, to hate the man she had married . . . remembering Randall, the boy he had loved and mourned, Kyre felt that he had to lay the blame for the apparent failure of that marriage at Sara's door . . .

Sara's child was born in the early hours of the morning, announcing its arrival with a loud, lusty cry which reached Kyre's ears as he sat by the dying fire, trying to read, yet conscious throughout the hours that he was awaiting the advent of the new life with some anxiety.

He was in the hall when Marsden came down, some half an hour later, smiling but weary, looking his age. There had been plenty of time for him to learn from Mrs. Nunhead that his patient was not Kyre Hamilton's wife, but the widow of the dead Randall Hamilton. So he adopted his manner accordingly.

'Well?' Kyre was impatient.

Marsden nodded. 'It's over. A boy weighing seven pounds and perfectly formed and healthy.'

'Mrs. Hamilton?'

'She's resting now. She's an extremely plucky young woman but she hasn't had an easy time. However, a good sleep will make her feel much better.' He was a little uneasy, remembering the way that his patient had turned away her head when Mrs. Nunhead brought the baby over, bathed and dressed and contented. He had brought many children into the world and was used to a new mother's eagerness for the first sight of her baby. Mrs. Hamilton's involuntary aversion and seeming indifference was unnatural and puzzling — but he comforted himself with the thought that it could only be a temporary frame of mind and that she would be as delighted with her son as any other mother when she had enjoyed her well-earned rest.

Kyre knew that tension seeped from him. He had not realised until that moment how tense, how anxious, how concerned he had been. 'Thank God!' he said fervently. He indicated the open door of his study. 'I've ordered coffee and sandwiches, Dr. Marsden.'

'Thank you . . . that's very kind.' He sighed briefly. 'I'll admit that they'll be very welcome.'

'May I see Mrs. Hamilton for a few minutes? Or is she asleep?'

'I've just given her a sedative. But it

takes a few minutes to work.' He pulled thoughtfully at his lip. 'I suppose there's no harm in a brief visit — but only a few minutes.'

'Thank you. Please make yourself comfortable. I'll be back very soon.' Kyre mounted the staircase slowly, wondering why he had made that impulsive request, why he wished to see Sara again that night. He had told her that he would visit her room the following day ... she would not be expecting him, might even resent his presence at such a time. He knocked lightly on the door and entered the room quietly, reluctant to disturb her if she were drowsy. She turned her head to look at him, her eyes shadowed with pain, her mouth tremulous.

Kyre crossed to the side of the bed, looked down at her reassuringly. 'Feeling better? I hear that you have a son — congratulations!'

'Thank you.' Her voice was dull, slurring with the effects of the sedative.

Carol, who had taken charge of the

baby, rose from her seat by the window. 'Would you like to see the baby, Kyre?'

He had been unaware of her presence and now he turned, startled. 'Oh . . . Carol.' He smiled. 'I expect you're delighted to have a baby to care for again, aren't you? Yes, I'd like to have a look at the boy.'

He crossed to the cot that had been hastily provided. He looked down at the sleeping baby . . . a soft fuzz of red-gold hair covered the small head and the features were as blurred and indistinct as that of most new-born infants. Yet Kyre, studying him intently, imagined a definite likeness to the Hamiltons in that tiny, peaceful face.

Sara watched him, her eyes inscrutable. His obvious interest in that tiny scrap of humanity was surprising — and oddly moving. For herself, she felt no interest in her baby. She had not wanted Randall's child any more than she had wanted him for a husband — and with the memory of her ordeal still so vivid she was devoid of any feeling of love for the cause of it all. She was thankful that it was over — and that was all. She felt numb, cold, indifferent.

Kyre came back to the bed. 'He's an attractive little beggar,' he said warmly. 'You must be very pleased. I mustn't stay. You're tired, I know — but I felt I'd like to see for myself that you were all right.' Meeting those grey, unemotional eyes, he felt embarrassed, uncomfortable, unnecessary. He did not blame her for being on the defensive. He was filled with compassion for this girl, still so young, who found herself in the position of a widow with a fatherless child. But he determined that she should not want for anything while he lived — and that her child should enjoy all the advantages that the Hamiltons had always known. He smiled down at her — and then, abruptly, impulsively, stooped to kiss her cheek. Swiftly, she averted her face from the touch of his lips — and the hot colour stormed to the roots of his hair at that unmistakable snub . . .

He went from the room, readily making allowances for her hostility, for her ungraciousness. He was a stranger to her, after all, despite their relationship by marriage . . . perhaps she were not used to demonstrations of affection that was motivated by the family tie.

Sara closed her eyes as the door closed gently behind him. She was grateful for his kindness, for his concern, for his warmth of manner — but she wanted none of it. He was a Hamilton and she meant to sever all connections with that family as soon as possible. She had good reason to fear and distrust anyone who bore the Hamilton name — and she did not want to become involved, no matter how loosely, how harmlessly, with any member of that family. There was no point in encouraging an unwelcome familiarity between them. She had hated and despised Randall and loathed the knowledge that she was to bear his child. Now, Randall was dead, the child had been born and there was nothing to keep her at Hamilton House once she was well enough to leave it . . .

The following morning, Kyre mounted the stairs, tall, lithe, energetic, despite having missed so much of his sleep. Dr. Marsden had just left him after making a routine call and he had assured Kyre that Sara would swiftly recover and be on her feet again. She seemed impatient to be up and about and that was always a good sign. He had betrayed an obvious curiosity about the new and unknown Mrs. Hamilton, but Kyre had adroitly side-stepped the subject.

As he walked along the corridor, Carol came out of Sara's room and he flashed her a swift, warm smile. The girl was pale and obviously weary. 'How is she?'

'Mrs. Hamilton seems quite well — but she's very listless,' she said smoothly. The tone of her voice did not betray the dislike and contempt she felt for the woman who took little or no interest in her own child.

'And the baby?'

Her eyes brightened for she loved children with all her heart. 'He's an angel! I wish he were mine!' she said impulsively.

Kyre smiled. 'It's about time you married and had children of your own, Carol. It isn't much fun looking after other people's infants all the time, surely?'

'Oh, I enjoy it,' she said sincerely. A faint dull flush touched her cheeks and her heart ached at the careless easy words. It seemed that he would never know how dear he was to her . . . that she only stayed at Hamilton House because she could be near to him . . . that she had made herself useful in other ways as soon as it became obvious that Vanessa would not need her much longer. Time and again, she told herself that she was being foolish, that she should get another job and leave this old, happy house and the man she loved, that Kyre Hamilton would never think of her as anything but the girl who cared for his sister's children. Time and again, the web in which she was so tightly enmeshed kept her at Hamilton House, within sight and sound of Kyre, and she found some small consolation in his friendly manner, the warmth of his smile, the easy intimacy of their brief conversations.

Throughout the night, sitting by the cot, watching and listening for the slightest sound which would tell her that the child or its mother needed her attentions, she had thought of Kyre and wondered at his interest and concern for the unknown girl who claimed to have married his cousin and, if likeness could be trusted, had borne his child. When he came to the room after the child was born, she had noted the kindliness, the warmth of his voice as he spoke to Sara and she had felt resentful jealousy and had broken in with a suggestion that he should look at the baby — if only that he should become aware that she was also in the room. She had been pierced with anguish as he stooped to kiss Sara before leaving — and known a malicious pleasure that he had been so coldly rebuffed even while her dislike for the girl had been heightened by the snub she had offered Kyre.

'You look all in,' Kyre said sympathetically. 'Why don't you get some sleep, Carol? Melanie or Cathryn can sit with Mrs. Hamilton — or Mrs. Nunhead if she isn't too busy.'

'Thank you . . . yes, I think I will go to bed for a few hours.' She managed a little laugh. 'It's so long since I sat up with Vanessa that I'd forgotten how long the night can be — and how difficult it is to keep awake.' She turned away and then back to him again: 'Oh . . . thank you for sending up the coffee and sandwiches, Kyre. It was very thoughtful of you.'

He hated to be thanked for something that, to him, had been a perfectly normal gesture, an appreciation, a consideration for someone in his employ. He brushed aside her thanks with a light remark and then watched her walk along the corridor. He hesitated briefly before knocking on the door of Sara's room.

'Oh . . . it's you!' Her tone was ungracious.

He ignored the lack of welcome in her voice. 'How are you this morning?'

'All right, thanks.'

'You're looking much better.'

She gave a little shrug. Kyre was puzzled by her hostile attitude. Even allowing for the fact that she had been hurt and disappointed in her marriage to Randall there seemed to be no reason why she should dislike and distrust him. He knew that he did not imagine her hostility. He went to look at the child. A smile touched his lips as he looked at the sleeping boy. Sara watched him coldly.

'You seem to like children.'

'Yes, I do,' he agreed. He turned to smile. 'You must be very proud of him, Sara. He's a beautiful child.'

'All babies look alike,' she returned indifferently.

'But not to their mothers,' he retorted swiftly. 'May I hold him for a moment?'

'He's asleep, isn't he?'

'Yes, I think so. Will he wake if I pick him up?'

'I don't know . . . possibly.'

He shook his head in bewilderment. Her tone conveyed so much indifference. Gently he lifted the child from the cot and cradled him in his arms. The boy stirred and the tiny face crumpled briefly.

Sara studied him curiously. The sight of her baby in his arms did not stir her to any emotion. She was merely surprised that he should show so much interest. He did not seem awkward, nor did he hold the child as though he feared to drop him.

'You have had practice in nursing babies,' she said.

He smiled. 'Not really. Melanie is a very modern mother and doesn't believe that babies should be nursed too much. I've not had much to do with children apart from Hamilton and Vanessa.'

'Really?' She drawled the word indifferently.

He was puzzled and irritated by her tone. But he persevered. 'You haven't met Melanie yet — my sister? You'll have plenty in common, anyway. She's a wonderful mother and she adores children — she'll be only too pleased to offer advice if you ask for it, Sara. I know she's looking forward to meeting you — and dying to see this little chap. Would you like her to sit with you for a while this morning?'

'I'm not in the mood for company.'

He walked to the bed, carrying the child. 'You'd better take him,' he said hastily as the movement roused the baby from sleep and again his face crumpled. He began to whimper.

Sara turned away abruptly. 'I don't want him. Put him back in the cot.'

He stared his astonishment. That deliberate aversion, that cold indifference to the cry of her child shocked him and, oddly, hurt him deeply. He knew that there were women who disliked and resented babies but he had always considered them to be unnatural and even abnormal. That a mother should turn from her own child was unthinkable to him.

'Maybe he needs changing,' he said uncertainly.

'He was changed a few minutes ago,' she returned coolly. 'If he is wet then he'll have to stay that way until Carol comes back.'

He tried to turn it into a joke. 'I'm no expert with babies, either. Nappy-changing isn't one of my specialities. But it must be fairly simple. Here, take him while I find a clean nappy . . . between us we'll sort out the way to do it.' His voice was urgent despite its light note.

'I told you . . . put him in the cot! I don't want anything to do with him!' There was a hint of near-hysteria in her voice.

The frail whimper become a demanding cry as though the child sensed the hostility of its mother. Kyre cradled him gently, soothing him with silly, tender crooning that eventually hushed him to sleep again. Sara lay rigid in the bed, her back to him, deliberately closing her ears to the sound of his gentle voice and her baby's cries. She knew that if she were to hold her child just once, study that small, helpless human being, she would be lost . . . that she could never walk out of this house and leave him behind . . . that she could not adhere to her determination to give him up entirely.

Kyre returned the baby to the cot, covered him with the blankets and touched the silky, delicate cheek briefly with his fingers. Poor little mite . . . fatherless, unwanted by his mother, a helpless, defenceless, vulnerable scrap of humanity.

He looked at Sara's resolute back — and swift anger flared in him. 'What's the matter with you?' he demanded. 'How can you be so unfeeling, so unnatural? Whatever your quarrel with

Randall, you can't take it out on an innocent baby!'

'Please leave me alone.'

He ran a hand through his thick, unruly hair. 'I don't understand you!'

'You don't know me!' she retorted, her voice muffled.

'I can't believe that you're really as indifferent to your own child as you pretend to be,' he told her fiercely.

'It isn't pretence. I didn't want him before he was born — and I don't want him now. I told you — there's no place for a baby in my life.'

'You should have thought of that before you went in for a child,' he told her grimly.

She turned at that, her eyes dark with loathing, her body trembling with the passion of her own anger. 'You don't know what you're talking about! This baby wasn't planned — or wanted! Even now, the memory of Randall's kisses, his arms about me, makes me shudder . . . I hated him to touch me. He wanted a child . . . I didn't! He was obsessed with the idea of bringing another Hamilton into the world. I wish I'd never married him!'

'Why did you?' His voice was icy, contemptuous.

She was suddenly quiet, controlled. She looked at him for a long moment. 'I repeat . . . you don't know what you're talking about,' she said stiffly.

'Then there seems little point in continuing this conversation,' he said coldly and walked to the door.

His anger was strong within him as he closed the door of his study and walked over to the decanters. Last night he had been sorry for the girl, almost liked her — now he felt that his compassion and liking had been misplaced, that he would be relieved when she left his house and they could forget the atmosphere of hostility and bitterness which she had brought with her.

He was calmer when his glass was empty. Foolish of him to lose his temper. The girl was overwrought, tired, emotional. She had suffered a severe shock on the previous day and given birth to her child only a few hours later. He must not attach too much importance to her words. Believing herself to be a deserted wife for all those months had made her bitter, distorted her outlook, turned her love for Randall into a contemptuous hatred. It would be better to pretend that their conversation had never taken place, ignore the implications of her remarks, allow for the upheaval of the last twenty-four hours and hope that her aversion to her child would be brief and temporary . . .

Melanie brushed that fine, pale hair into smoothness, conscious that her ministrations were resented, and puzzled by the evident hostility. She had helped Sara into one of her own more practical nightgowns, held the mirror while she listlessly applied powder and lipstick and then offered to brush her hair.

Sara was silent. She supposed she should be grateful that Melanie had sacrificed her own pleasures to keep her company and attend to her needs. Melanie had entered, announcing her identity, begging to see the baby, a tall, attractive, self-possessed woman with an easy warmth of manner and a pleasant friendliness. She had scarcely listened while Melanie rhapsodised over her child's red-gold hair, the deep blue of his eyes, the pink and white skin and delicate features, the chubbiness of arms and legs.

Melanie put down the brush. 'That's better,' she said lightly. 'You have lovely hair . . . such a pretty, unusual colour. Now, can I get anything for you?'

'No, thank you.'

'Sure?' Melanie wandered over to the cot. 'He's sleeping like an angel, bless him.' Her voice held the tenderness of a woman who was herself a mother and loved all children. She turned to smile at Sara. 'What are you going to call him?'

'I haven't thought about it.'

'Oh . . . well, there's plenty of time.' Melanie hesitated and then said gently, compassionately: 'I suppose you wouldn't want to give him Randall's name . . . ?'

'No!' The exclamation was fierce, vehement.

Melanie cursed herself for her lack of tact. It had been thoughtless, even cruel — for Sara had only learned the day before of Randall's death and she must be suffering an agony of heartache.

Sara had trained herself not to think about Randall during the past six months — now she regretted the impulse which had brought her to this house in time for the birth of her child. There were too many reminders of him . . . too many people who had not known the real Randall, who had loved him and mourned him with sincerity . . . too many difficult situations that were likely to arise during her short stay with his family.

'Does it . . . hurt too much — to talk about him?' Melanie spoke quietly.

'Hurt? No, it doesn't hurt,' Sara returned dully.

Melanie came to sit on the edge of

the bed. 'My dear, I wish I could tell you how deeply we all feel for you. Randall . . . he was such a dear boy — so full of life. Everyone loved him. It's terrible for you, Sara — but please believe that we all want to be your friends, to help you in any way we can. After all,' she smiled, 'you are our cousin now, aren't you? Part of the family.'

Sara writhed inwardly. She could not tolerate the gentle compassion in Melanie's voice, the obvious sincerity of her words. She did not want to suffer their pity, to enjoy their kindness and friendliness, to accept their hospitality on false pretences. It was natural enough that the Hamiltons should assume that she had been in love with Randall, that she mourned the loss of her husband — but she could not bear to have them talk of him so affectionately, so tenderly. It was obvious that they knew nothing of his way of life. They did not know, as she did, that he was capable of abominable behaviour, of treachery and mockery and deceit, of cruel and calculated . . . blackmail!

'Thank you,' she said flatly. 'But . . . do you mind — if we don't talk of Randall.'

Melanie was all concern. 'Oh, my dear, I've upset you! Kyre will never forgive me! I am sorry!'

'No, I'm not upset,' she said firmly. 'But I'd rather not talk about the past. It's over and done with now.'

Melanie nodded. 'I do understand,' she said gently. 'But remember . . . we want to do anything we can to help you, to make you welcome, to make you feel that you really belong to the family now.' She rose to her feet. 'Do you think you could sleep a little? Are you quite comfortable?'

'Yes, thank you. You've been very kind.' But there was no emotion, no gratitude in her voice. She lay back on her pillows and closed her eyes.

6

Melanie slipped quietly from the room. After a momentary hesitation, she went in search of her brother and found him just leaving the house.

'Oh, Kyre . . . can you spare a minute?'

He turned immediately. 'Of course! Is anything wrong?'

'No. It's just that I want to talk to you about Sara,' she explained.

'Sara . . . yes. What do you think of her?'

She wrinkled her brow. 'I'm not sure. I'm a bit puzzled, Kyre, I'd like to feel sorry for her . . . there's reason enough, heaven knows — but she seems so calm, so unemotional, so . . . untouched by everything. She won't talk about Randall — and I wish I could think she was heartbroken. But she doesn't give that impression.'

'No,' he agreed slowly.

'She doesn't seem at all interested in her baby,' Melanie went on, almost indignantly. 'He's a lovely little boy — but she won't even look at him and says that she has no intention of feeding him herself! It's really very strange.'

'Perhaps she's still feeling the after-effects, Melanie. It's a fairly usual reaction, isn't it? She'll soon get over it.'

'I hope so,' she said doubtfully. 'It's terrible to lose your husband before your child is born — but in those circumstances I should have thought that it was more natural for a woman to take some comfort from the baby.'

'And she doesn't?'

'She ignores him completely — and seems quite content to let someone else look after him. I really don't understand it, Kyre.'

He smiled. 'Neither do I, my dear but I expect things will sort themselves out.' He gave a weary gesture. 'I wish we'd known about Randall's marriage when it happened. I find this all rather disconcerting and tiresome.'

He was, in truth, a little bored with the subject of Sara and her baby. It seemed that he had done nothing that day but ward off questions and wriggle out of discussions. Everyone seemed to expect him to deal with the matter capably — and, so far as he could see, there was really nothing that needed his administration. Sara was Randall's widow and a member of the family. If she wanted to stay at Hamilton House she was welcome to do so: if she chose to leave and take her child with her, there was nothing he could do about it. Privately, remembering his conversation with her earlier that day, he would be thankful if she chose to leave and the house could return to normal.

Sara was grateful to be left alone — for the first time, it seemed, since she had arrived at this big, forbidding, vaguely frightening house. Everyone was being kind — too kind, too sympathetic, too tactful, she thought bitterly. If only they knew how little she needed their sympathy or their tact!

So Randall was dead — and the girl who had been forced to take his name and bear his child could not feel any sorrow or regret. His supposed desertion had been a relief although it had left certain complications in its wake — his death was an even greater relief. She did not intend to play the part of a hypocrite for anyone — let the family she had married into think what they chose about her lack of feeling!

She had not been particularly impressed by the few members of the family that she had met. Perhaps she had been prejudiced by Randall's frequent comments — he had enjoyed caricaturing them and expounding their faults and failings and sneering at their loves and loyalties and lack of initiative.

Kyre had been kind and considerate, she granted — but she could not help thinking of him in the light of the head of the family, the autocrat, the dominant force, the holder of the purse-strings, the successful and probably conceited author.

Randall's sister, Cathryn, had been pleasant enough, but Sara had sensed the resentment and the incredulity behind the façade of sympathy and friendliness.

Melanie had been slightly patronising, due no doubt to her extra years, her experiences of motherhood and her ill-concealed conviction that Sara's present aversion to her child would soon be replaced by a more natural affection and eagerness and pride.

The door opened gently. Sara knew a sudden spurt of annoyance. Couldn't they leave her in peace? No light of warmth or welcome touched her eyes as she looked at the old, silver-haired lady who hesitated doubtfully on the threshold.

'Am I disturbing you my dear? Shall I go away?' she asked timidly.

'No, it's all right.' She suppressed a sigh.

Dimity Hamilton moved softly across

the room to the side of the bed. 'I've been so curious about you,' she admitted with the naïvety of a young girl.

'I expect they all are,' she replied coolly.

'Oh, yes.' Aunt Dimity looked at Sara wonderingly. 'You're very young, my dear,' she said in surprise. 'And very pretty.'

Sara laughed harshly. The mirror had reflected a face marked with suffering and bitterness and discontent — and she had not cared. 'You must be Randall's aunt,' she said and suppressed the memory of Randall's words; '*She's slightly off her rocker but quite harmless, poor old girl — living in the big house all one's life is enough to send anyone round the bend, I should think.*'

Aunt Dimity beamed. 'Oh, did Randall tell you about me? We were devoted to each other, you know. The dear boy — such a loss to us all . . . ' She sighed. 'But I mustn't make you sad, my dear or Kyre will be cross with me. May I have the tiniest peep at your little baby?'

'Yes, of course,' she said indifferently.

With exaggerated care and quietness, Aunt Dimity tiptoed to the cot and bent over the sleeping baby. Her sweet and oddly youthful face was illumined with a tenderness that should have been touching but only served to irritate Sara.

'He's beautiful — and so like his poor dear father.'

'I hope not,' Sara muttered to herself.

Aunt Dimity glanced at her. Her ears were keener than most people realised and her eyes narrowed shrewdly. She had already come to the conclusion that there was more to this odd marriage of Randall's than seemed on the surface — and she had overheard enough snippets of conversation to know that the family were puzzled by the girl's strange aversion to her child and her seeming indifference to her husband's death. Mrs. Nunhead would not dream of speaking her mind on such a delicate subject to any member of the family but she confided freely in Jeffries, her particular crony — and Aunt Dimity's ears were very keen. She knew that she had the reputation of being not only vague but also lacking in mental alertness and efficiency — a reputation born of a veil of mystery and secrecy drawn discreetly over a long-forgotten scandal and substantiated by Dimity's own withdrawal into herself throughout the years. But she was no fool and she had a keener perception and under-standing than most realised.

She cooed over the baby for a few minutes and then left the cot and drew a chair closer to the bed. 'A lovely little baby,' she sighed. 'A true Hamilton. You mustn't mind that he looks like his father, my dear. Looks aren't everything — it's character that counts. Poor Randall was sadly lacking in that, of course — a weak strain in him, I'm afraid.' She shook her head. 'I never did care for his mother, you know — a lovely woman but cold and hard and calculating. She led poor Martin a lively dance. He loved this house but he didn't dare to stay here while Kay travelled all over the place — he couldn't trust her, you see, my dear.'

'Really?' Sara was bored. She could not see that the revelations about Randall's long-dead mother could have any bearing on the present.

Aunt Dimity produced her knitting from the bag that she carried everywhere with her. Sara gritted her teeth. It seemed as though the old woman was settling down for a long session!

'This is a little coat for the baby,' Aunt Dimity said, holding up the white piece of knitting. 'I happened to have some wool by me.'

'Thank you . . . but he has lots of clothes,' Sara said, not caring that she might sound ungracious. She thought wearily of the long evenings, alone in the small, shabby flat, conscious of a chill that the fitful gas fire could not disperse, when she had occupied her hands and her mind with knitting and sewing for the child she did not want.

The needles began to click industriously. 'Randall was very like his mother. He liked things to his way. He could not be thwarted — even as a child — and he would scheme and connive and cajole — and even blackmail at times to get his own way.' Aunt Dimity looked up with a sweet, innocent smile. 'The child is the father of the man — isn't that the saying? Randall grew up exactly the same — liking his own way, determined to have it, pushing aside all obstacles.'

Sara was silent. She did not know if the old lady was trying to draw her to talk of Randall, to criticise him, to admit that she had seen signs of those things in him — but she did wonder why Dimity Hamilton should be talking in such vein. Could she sense Sara's own harsh thoughts about her husband? Did she know, in some strange way, that Sara had hated Randall — and want Sara to understand that she knew and appreciated her reasons.

'He loved money too much,' Aunt Dimity went on gently. 'That was the crux of the whole matter. Martin was the youngest son. Kay thought she was marrying money and took her disappointment very badly. Randall grew up in the belief that he would be a wealthy young man — and he was impatient for the handling of the supposed wealth. Money meant everything to him. He was beside himself with rage when my brother died and he learned that the house, the estate and the family income were entailed — and that Kyre, as the eldest son of the eldest son, naturally inherited everything. Kyre was always very generous — but it was never enough. Randall had extravagant tastes, you see . . .'

'Why are you telling me all this?' Sara broke in impatiently. She did not need to be told that Randall put money before everything else!

Aunt Dimity looked vaguely startled. 'You're one of the family now, my dear. You should know these things. And no one else will tell you. You see, we all loved Randall despite his faults — and since his death he has been loved because of his faults. No one else will ever say a word against him. But he wasn't a very nice person, my dear. Oh, charming and good-looking and vital, intelligent and good-humoured, affectionate and lovable — but cruel. He had that cruel streak in him just like his mother. I expect you knew he was cruel?'

'Yes', Sara said dully. 'I knew.'

Aunt Dimity nodded sagely. 'I thought you must. But it really wasn't his fault. He had the wrong mother — and he was such a wilful and spoiled little boy. We all loved him too much. You mustn't make that mistake with your little boy . . . ' She broke off as the door opened.

Kyre was surprised to see his aunt. He smiled. 'I thought you might be alone, Sara. But I see that Aunt Dimity has been keeping you company. Are you all right?'

'I'm fine, thanks. Just bored with being in bed.'

He laughed. 'So soon. Well, you'll soon be out of it.'

Aunt Dimity gathered up her knitting. 'I must be going. I've so many things to do.' She patted Sara's hand gently and smiled. 'You won't forget the things I've told you, my dear. Character is so important, you see — and it begins to form in the earliest days. You must check the bad before it becomes impossible to control.'

Kyre lifted his eyebrows and smiled. 'That sounds very ominous, Aunt Dimity.'

His aunt sailed across the room with a quaint, old-fashioned dignity. 'I'm just a silly old woman, Kyre — but I haven't lived in this world for seventy-eight years without learning a few things about human nature.'

Courteously, Kyre held the door for his aunt and then closed it gently behind her. He smiled at Sara. 'What on earth have you two been talking about?'

he asked lightly.

'Human nature,' she retorted coolly.

'Aunt Dimity been giving you good advice? What do you think of her? She's a sweet old dear, don't you think? And not so vague as you might think.'

'Oh, I don't think she's vague,' Sara returned quietly. She knew that Aunt Dimity had been trying to tell her something important in her roundabout way and she was irritated by Kyre's unwelcome intrusion. He wandered over to the cot.

'He sleeps a lot, doesn't he?'

'I thought all babies slept most of the time.'

'I suppose they do.' He turned to smile. 'You seem to be having plenty of visitors.'

She nodded. She did not want to talk to him. She wanted to be alone to think over her conversation with Aunt Dimity.

'Is it too early to ask if you have any plans for the future?' he asked carefully.

She met his eyes steadily, almost scornfully. 'I told you yesterday what my plans were. Don't worry, I haven't changed my mind. I've no intention of imposing on your hospitality any longer than necessary.'

'I don't want you to think that your presence here is an imposition,' he said swiftly. 'You're very welcome to stay indefinitely. This is open house to any member of the family.'

'So I've been told,' she said drily. 'There's quite a medieval atmosphere about the place.'

Faint dull colour touched his cheeks. 'You don't approve?'

She shrugged. 'It isn't my business.'

He walked to the window and thrust his hands into his pockets. 'It may not have occurred to you that I find it more economical to have all my family under one roof. Perhaps Randall never explained the medieval arrangement that only the head of the family is considered responsible enough to hold the purse-strings. The family income has dwindled considerably since the entail was set up — and it would be quite a drain on me to provide sufficient funds for everyone to have their own roof over their heads and to live in comparative comfort.'

He was a little surprised that he should be so frank with this girl. He had never before, even to Honor, explained his reluctance to persuade Uncle James or Aunt Dimity or even Melanie and Philip to leave the protection of Hamilton House.

Sara stared at his tall, uncompromising figure. 'They must have some money of their own!'

He turned to look at her. 'A little — but not enough.'

'Your sister's husband — couldn't he get a job?' Her tone was faintly contemptuous.

'Philip? He's an artist.'

'I know — but not a very successful artist,' Sara said smoothly.

'His approach is still very new. In a few years time he'll probably be famous and rich,' Kyre said, smiling.

'But he may not be! Do you intend to

support them and their children indefinitely?'

'As long as I can afford to do so.' He spoke coldly now, resenting the mockery behind her words.

'What happens when Cathryn gets married? Will you keep her husband and children too?'

He shrugged. 'If necessary. She may find herself a wealthy husband.'

'And your brother?'

He laughed. 'Is this an inquisition? Kane earns his keep, believe me. I'm grateful to him for taking on the estate work. It means that I am free to write.'

'Your uncle and aunt . . . they might live for years yet!'

He stiffened. 'I hope they do, Sara. You seem to think that I find my family an intolerable burden on my finances. I haven't yet been reduced to selling the family heirlooms to keep us all, you know. The bills are paid on time, we live comfortably and eat well and even entertain on occasions. You mustn't imagine that the bailiffs are sitting on the doorstep!'

She smiled reluctantly. 'Not yet, perhaps. But it must be only a matter of time.' She was abruptly thoughtful. 'Randall must have known how matters stood.'

'Of course.'

Her mouth tightened as she remembered her husband's scathing comment: '*The tight old buzzard gives me a mere pittance and keeps his hands firmly on the money that's mine by right. Well, he'll have to fork out to keep you and the kid — and I'll see that he does.*'

'He only had what you allowed him?'

He sensed criticism in her voice. 'I did my best,' he said sharply. 'He grew up thinking that money was there for the asking — and he never had to ask where I was concerned. He ran up bills all over London and sent them to me — and they were always paid without question. Youngsters are always extravagant and naturally they don't want to worry whether or not the money is available to pay for their pleasures.'

Sara wondered briefly if the bills that seemed to arrive with monotonous regularity during her short sojourn with Randall and which were always stuffed into his pocket with a careless mention of settling them the next day had been forwarded to Kyre Hamilton and paid by him. Certainly Randall had always grumbled about lack of money and warned her against extravagance — yet never lacked the money to buy drink and cigarettes, to pay for the lavish parties he loved to throw, to play the generous, genial and popular host to an assortment of friends at nightclubs and restaurants, to order new suits and shoes — or to buy the expensive sports car he had wanted and naturally obtained. Sara had known where the money for these things came from, of course — and her lip curled contemptuously at the thought.

She had provided their food and daily necessities and put aside for emergencies the remainder of the salary she was receiving for her small part in the play at the *Minerva*. Later she was to be thankful for her forethought when she could no longer work and had no husband to support her.

It had not been difficult to believe that Randall had deliberately walked out on their marriage when an apologetic agent explained that the rent for their flat had not been paid for a month and that unless it was forthcoming she would have to leave. She had told Randall at the time that the luxurious flat was an expense they could not afford and he had assured her that he would attend to such things. Knowing that she could not afford to pay the high rent out of her salary, Sara had gathered together her few possessions and found herself a small bed-sitting-room. Her landlady had been curious and obviously doubtful of the existence of the husband that Sara claimed to be abroad but she had been kind enough as long as the rent was paid regularly.

With her resources steadily dwindling, Sara had remembered her promise to Randall to have her child at his family home — and it had seemed the solution to a problem. But she had not expected to hear that Randall was dead — and it was natural enough to wonder if he would have kept the vows of their marriage if he had lived . . . if he had been on his way to make arrangements for them to live at Hamilton House — or if he had no intention of coming back for her if he had not been killed. She did not doubt the Hamiltons' assertion that they had never heard of her despite Randall's assurance that he had written to his cousin Kyre. The lack of an answer had been airily shrugged aside with the cynical comment that Kyre probably didn't welcome the thought of handing over sufficient funds to provide for Sara and the coming child but that he would come round in time. She knew only too well that Randall had an answer for anything and cared little for the truth.

The love that Randall had claimed to

have for her had been nothing more than a physical passion which might have been his only capacity for loving. It had not long survived the reluctant surrender to his demands. She could believe that he had been pleased that she was going to have his child — supreme egotist that he was, he welcomed the thought of a being cast in his mould, a child that he had propagated . . . for Sara knew that he gave her little credit for her condition. She had not been pleased except for the hope that their child might cement their mockery of a marriage into something more worthwhile, more lasting, more tolerable.

The knowledge that Randall was dead was the gateway to freedom. She had no interest in his son and felt no scruples about leaving him to the care, financial and moral and physical, of the quixotic Kyre Hamilton. Her only thought for the future was to return to the theatre as soon as possible. She would never marry again even if the opportunity came her way — one experience of marriage was enough. Perhaps every man was not like Randall — but she did not propose to take the chance.

7

She had been silent for so long that Kyre glanced at her curiously, noting the hard gleam of her eyes and the faint, scornful curl of her lips. He wondered of what she was thinking . . . and then the baby in the cot woke abruptly and began to cry — the plaintive, demanding cry of hunger.

Kyre looked uncertainly from Sara to the cot. Did she feel any differently about her baby now? Or would she again refuse to hold him, to concern herself about him?

Sara clenched her hands involuntarily. 'What's wrong with him?'

Kyre was startled. 'I thought mothers always knew the answer.'

'Well, I don't,' she said fiercely.

'Maybe he's hungry.'

'Then you'd better find Carol. She's supposed to be his nurse, isn't she?'

The baby's crying became louder and more demanding, more piteous. Kyre stooped over the cot. 'I'd better pick him up.'

Sara was conscious of the heaviness of milk in her breasts — an almost painful awareness. 'Oh, damn you! Give him to me!' she snapped. 'And get out.'

Hastily he lifted the baby and brought him over to the bed. Her arms went out to take her son and curved about him with a natural, easy tenderness. He butted his small, downy head against her breast and his mouth automatically moved to suck on the empty air. Sara looked down at him and something hard and cold within her seemed to melt and disappear in that moment. She drew him against her and touched the gentle curve of his cheek, almost in wonder. Kyre moved towards the door, a faint smile touching his lips. Nature had solved the problem, after all, he thought, pleased . . .

Carol came hurrying into the room some minutes later. She paused in surprise. 'Oh, you're feeding him!' she exclaimed in genuine pleasure.

'I didn't have any choice in the matter,' Sara retorted. She resented the girl's intrusion for she had been studying the minute perfections of her son and crooning gently to him while he concentrated single-mindedly on the most important thing in his young life.

'He looks bloated,' Carol said, smiling. 'I think he's had enough this time, Mrs. Hamilton. Shall I change him and put him down?'

'Not yet. I want to hold him for a little while.' There was a faint defiance in her tone as she dared the girl to remind her of her former indifference.

'I'll come back later, shall I?' Carol suggested tactfully and went from the room.

Within minutes, the family knew of Sara's change of heart.

'It was inevitable,' Melanie said, a little smugly.

'The poor child has had a lot to bear,' Aunt Dimity reminded her gently.

'Hm! I should think so! Never heard such nonsense in my life!' growled Uncle James.

'Mothers!' Philip interrupted his brushwork to exclaim scornfully with a cast of his eyes to the heavens.

'I can't imagine why she changed her mind,' Honor drawled indifferently. 'Bottle-feeding is so much more convenient — and less messy.'

'Well, that's her affair, isn't it?' Kane paused briefly to add to the general discussion before making his way to the study.

Kyre looked up from his typewriter. 'I thought you were out. Do you want me?'

'I want to glance through the accounts for last month,' he said, trotting out his ready excuse for the interruption.

Kyre nodded towards the file on its shelf. 'Go ahead.'

Kane made a pretence of studying the file. 'What are you going to do about that girl?' he asked carelessly.

'Sara?'

'Yes. Mrs. Randall Hamilton.'

'What do you expect me to do? She'll make up her own mind,' Kyre said with faint impatience.

'Will you encourage her to stay and live off the fat of the land provided by you and me?'

'Why not?'

'Can you afford it?' Kane asked bluntly.

Kyre ran his hands through his dark hair. 'Everyone seems suddenly concerned about money? I could afford to pay for Randall's extravagances — I imagine it must be cheaper to keep Sara and her child!'

'She's an actress, I believe.' Kyre nodded and his twin's lips curled in a faint sneer. 'If Randall thought her a good actress then she isn't likely to go back to the profession. His taste and understanding were sorely lacking in that respect,' Kane drawled.

Kyre pushed back his chair and rose to his feet. 'What's wrong? Don't you want the girl to stay here?'

'What makes you think she will fit into this household?'

'Why shouldn't she? Philip has settled down well enough,' Kyre reminded him.

'Philip has his painting and would be happy in a barn as long as food and clothing and painting materials were provided free of charge!'

Kyre grinned. 'True enough.' He glanced at his twin and was surprised by a look of uneasiness in those usually inscrutable dark eyes. 'What's bothering you?'

He shook his head. 'Nothing,' he hedged. 'I merely feel that you've been imposed on enough without having another two mouths to feed.'

Kyre rested a hand on Kane's shoulder for a brief moment. 'I'm medieval in my outlook,' he said, smiling. 'I like my family under one roof.'

'You're a glutton for responsibility,' Kane retorted. He thrust his hand into his pocket and brought out a thick wad of bills. 'This little lot arrived this morning,' he said, dropping them one by one on the desk.

Kyre shrugged. 'It's the end of the month.'

Kane smiled reluctantly. 'I have to admire you, Kyre. You never turn a hair, do you?'

'Not since I had this letter from Purbrook this morning,' Kyre said and there was a note of excitement in his voice as he handed a sheet of notepaper to his brother.

Kane scanned it rapidly. Then he looked up, gave a little whistle and proceeded to read it again. 'Well, that's a nice turn-up for the book,' he said in surprise. 'Congratulations!'

Kyre accepted the return of the letter and replaced it in his breast pocket. 'Yes . . . I knew it was in the wind but I didn't care to mention it until it was settled. Purbrook is a good agent and he's held out for the best price.'

'Does that mean you'll be rushing

over to America to supervise the filming?'

'I doubt it very much. The book will probably be mutilated out of all recognition and I'd rather not have any responsibility for the final result. I don't suppose critical authors are very welcome in film studios, anyway.'

'Eighty-five thousand dollars — it's a lot of money, Kyre.'

'More than it's worth — but I'm not going to tell them so,' he said, grinning. 'If you've been postponing the happy event because you thought I couldn't afford to keep you *and* a wife then you can go ahead without worrying now.'

Kane laughed. 'I'm a bachelor and shall remain so till the end of my days,' he prophesied. 'I've enough on my plate without a woman to worry about. I must get back. We're re-fencing Lower Lea and Saunders came in search of me to check my orders for last month from Garfields. See you later, twin.'

On his way across the hall, he caught sight of Honor at the writing-bureau in the sitting-room. He swung lithely on his heel and entered the room. She looked up with an absent smile and then returned to her letters. Kane stood behind her chair, looking down at that sleek, arrogant head, anger tearing through him that she should dismiss him so casually. Abruptly he stooped and kissed the back of her neck with a sudden fierceness.

'Ouch!' she exclaimed impatiently. 'Kane — you'll mark my neck!'

'Good!' he said savagely.

She twisted in her chair to look up at him. 'What on earth is wrong with you?'

He lounged against the bureau and folded his strong, bare arms across his chest. 'My big brother has just given me his permission to find myself a wife. How about it?' His eyes were dark and inscrutable, his mouth twisted slightly into a faint sneer.

'An excellent idea,' she said calmly. 'It's time you were married and gave up pestering me.'

His hand clamped down abruptly on

her shoulder, so fiercely that she cried with pain. 'Don't treat me like the carpet beneath your feet,' he said savagely. 'I'm a man — more of a man than my excellent brother will ever be — as you'd find out if you were to relax for five minutes when I'm around.'

'Really, Kane, I'm not in the mood for your nonsense,' she said, struggling to evade his clasp. 'I've letters to write.'

'Damn your letters.' With a swift movement he sent notepaper, envelopes and pen flying from the desk to the floor. She stared up at him, frightened by the glimpse of savagery in his make-up yet oddly exalted by the knowledge that she could stir him to fierce emotion. She meant to marry Kyre but she enjoyed playing with fire — and Kane was fiery to the core. She knew he wanted her . . . she would not gloss it with the fine gossamer of love — she was under no illusions as to the nature of the passion that she moved in him.

'You'd better get back to your fields,'

she taunted. 'Your muddy boots are scarcely suited for the house.'

'And my muddy hands mustn't soil your beautiful body?' he retorted and raised her by the shoulders until she stood facing him, nearly as tall as himself, proud and beautiful and contemptuous of his strength and passion. 'I'll be your master yet, Honor,' he said grimly. 'Kyre will never marry you — and if you wait much longer you'll be thankful to marry a man like me!'

'And be dependent on Kyre's charity? That isn't for me, my dear,' she said arrogantly.

'You've money of your own!'

She smiled faintly. 'Have I?'

'So you've always led us to believe,' he reminded her.

'A thousand a year,' she told him. 'Scarcely enough for my clothes. Why do you think I spend my time living in other people's houses? Has it never occurred to you that I'm never to be found at the luxurious flat that I claim to rent in London?'

'A thousand a year with my allowance will keep us both comfortably,' he said fiercely.

'Your ideas of comfort must differ from mine,' she drawled. 'You must be mad to think I'd marry you when your brother has so much more to offer.'

He caught her against him and kissed her savagely until she was breathless. 'Can he offer this?' he demanded. His hands were demanding and oddly exciting. 'Or this?' His lips were hot on her throat and then on her shoulder as he wrenched away the thin wool dress and then they travelled gently, insistently to her breast. 'Can he make you feel like a woman?' he asked urgently as he felt her quiver within his arms. 'I'm damned if he can; You're my woman, Honor — and don't forget it!'

With these words, he released her, so abruptly that she staggered, and grinned at her mockingly before turning on his heel and striding from the room.

Flushed, her hair coming loose from

its sleek chignon, aware of the uncontrollable trembling of her body, Honor caught at the torn material of her dress. She had never been more angry in her life — but mixed with the anger was that same feeling of exultation that he could always bring to life, a fierce heat in her veins and an awareness that he stirred her to greater passion that she had ever experienced in the arms of other men . . .

Kane Hamilton, a forceful, passionate man with the hot blood of the Hamiltons in his veins, strode across the fields towards Lower Lea. The biting chill of the day invigorated him and he was still warmed by the memory of Honor's slim and lovely body in his arms. He had known many women but none had ever stirred him so deeply, so lastingly, as Honor and he was determined that she would eventually marry him. He knew that she was selfish and wilful, cold and hard: he knew that he was the one man to make her forget self, to break that strong will, to breathe life and fire into her cold heart and melt that hard core with the weakness and surrender of wanting. It might be generally accepted that one day she would be Kyre's wife — but Kane did not fear his brother's charms. He loved and respected Kyre and would not deliberately harm him but he did not think that the loss of Honor would be such a blow to his twin. Once he had thought so and had practised caution and deceit in his passionate wooing — and lived to regret it, he thought now with a sudden twist of his lips. He had never nursed illusions about Honor. He knew that she was determined to marry money and would never consider him as a husband while Kyre held the purse-strings and had no choice but to be financially responsible for his family. For some time, he had been accumulating money in devious ways and soon he would have enough to sway Honor's mercenary heart. He could live with his conscience — and life was easier now that Randall was dead. But he had taken a wife and Kane had been restless ever since he learned of her presence at Hamilton House, wondering how much she knew about the family into which she had married, how much she knew about Randall's tendency towards blackmail . . .

Aunt Dimity stared into the fire, her usually busy hands lying idle in her lap, the knitting on the floor by her feet. Despite the blaze of heat from the burning logs, she was shivering and her eyes were introspective as her thoughts flew down the years to recall the terror and the shame. For six months, she had been at peace for the first time in years — but now this young girl with the bitter eyes and the secret knowledge in her heart had come to Hamilton House to bring a recurrence of dread and worry. She had married Randall — and he had been a braggart with a careless tongue. Was it all to start again? Was this girl tarred with the same brush? Did she have a dark motive for coming to this house? Had she known that Randall was dead and, having reason to hate and despise him, decided to take a sweet revenge against his family? One member of that family, in particular? Aunt Dimity closed her eyes with a little sigh and thought wearily of the long years . . . would it matter if her long-kept secret came to light now? Had she really committed such a grievous sin? It was all such a long time ago . . .

Uncle James stamped up and down his bedroom, a deep frown furrowing his brow, chewing his moustache anxiously. The girl was an impostor! Randall had married her — a likely story! The boy had liked his freedom . . . liked too many women . . . liked money too much! Kyre must send her packing at the earliest moment — and the brat too! It was too much at his time of life to cope with the fear that the girl's story might be true, that she might have been told the secret that James Hamilton had struggled so long to keep from the family. Randall had never been trustworthy — a sly, mercenary, inquisitive young imp with a smile to charm the heart out of Satan himself and a way of getting what he wanted with the minimum of effort. No doubt he had boasted that he could always lay his hands on the money he liked so much ... that there were ways and means ... that almost everyone had a secret locked away that they would not want publicised. Randall had always had the flair for learning these things and even as a small child he had been swift to learn the advantages ... sweets, extra pocket money, denied confidences — and always with that belying innocent smile, a light-hearted quip, a show of affection that caused one to wonder if he *realised* that his cajolery was nothing more than blackmail ...

Melanie smoked a cigarette with quick, disturbed puffs, exasperated by her husband's quiet, casual indifference to their predicament.

'Don't you understand?' she demanded impatiently. 'If Randall told her ...'

He looked up absently from the mixing of colours on his palette. 'Why should he have told her, darling?'

She threw her cigarette into the fire angrily. 'Oh! Because Randall could never keep a still tongue in his head — unless he was paid to do so! And she must have wondered why he was so affluent when he had so little money of his own! Of couse he must have told her where the money came from!'

'Well, we didn't give him that much,' he said patiently.

'More than we could afford to give him!' she snapped. 'Anyway, perhaps we weren't the only ones — even as a kid, he always seemed to be hugging secrets to himself and there was that look in his eyes that hinted that he knew more than he was telling . . . at the moment!'

'I still think we should have told him to go to hell. It's ancient history, darling.'

Her eyes blazed. 'Would you want your children to grow up knowing that . . . ' She broke off. She could not bring the words into the open — neither of them had ever done so since that night when Philip had told her about his past, not knowing that Randall was in the vicinity and listening avidly to every word.

He put down his palette and hurried to take her in his arms. 'I agreed to pay him to keep quiet for your sake, Melanie,' he said. 'I never thought it was the wise thing to do. A clip on the jaw would have been more effective — and if he'd chosen to spout about my past it couldn't have done much harm . . . '

'Don't talk such rubbish! If he'd talked to the right people you'd have been hauled off to prison,' she reminded him.

He was silent for a long moment. 'Okay . . . so we paid him and he kept quiet. It was worth it, wasn't it?'

She cradled his face in her hands. 'Yes, it was worth it, Philip. But I don't want it to start all over again — the constant demands, the innuendoes, the horrible fear that he'd want more next time . . .'

He held her away from him abruptly, fiercely. 'What do you mean? We only gave him that five hundred!'

She shook her head. 'No . . . '

He searched her face intently. 'You gave him more?'

Melanie nodded wearily.

'How much?'

She turned away from him. 'I can't remember — too much, I expect. He was always in debt . . . and it was always the last time.' She gave a little shudder.

'The little rat!'

A faint smile touched her lips. 'Yes, I suppose he was, Philip. Blackmail . . . it's a horrible word, isn't it? And a horrible occupation. But it never seemed like blackmail, somehow. He was always so sweet and affectionate — it always seemed as though he was asking a favour and one didn't have the heart to refuse him. Odd how you can go on loving someone even when they're asking you for money . . . money that we wanted for the children.'

'I admit he was a likeable devil — but I'd have wrung his neck if I'd known that he was pestering for more. It was worth five hundred to me to stay here with you and the kids, to know that I was safe — but it certainly wasn't worth your peace of mind. That car crash was a stroke of luck for us!'

She turned on him quickly. 'Don't say things like that! He was young with the rest of his life before him . . . it wasn't his fault that money was his god — he'd been brought up thinking that he'd inherit a fortune . . .'

'For God's sake — don't make excuses for him, Melanie. Your family are all besotted about Randall — to listen to any one of you, one would think he was a man above men! He had charm and intelligence and a warm personality, maybe — I couldn't help liking him as much as anyone. But I don't gild the lily. He was a blackmailing little swine — and he enjoyed having people in his power.'

Melanie sighed. 'Well, he's dead now and can't do any more harm. I have you and the children — and the money doesn't really matter.'

He stared at her. 'Are you content to live here for the rest of your life, then? Don't you ever want a house of your own, decent schools for the kids, a different way of life?'

'Kyre . . . ' she began but he interrupted fiercely.

'I'm sick of being kept by my brother in law! And I don't want my son's education to be paid for by anyone but myself! Is that so difficult to understand?'

She stiffened, resenting his anger. 'Then you'd better try painting something that people will buy, my dear! You've been virtually kept by Kyre for seven years and this is the first time I've known you to raise any objections! Maybe your work will be appreciated a hundred years hence — but it certainly wouldn't feed and clothe us now if we left this house!'

She turned on her heel and swung from the room, her eyes stinging with angry tears. They rarely quarrelled and she knew her words had hurt him — bitterly she blamed everything on the girl who had come to the house to stir old, dead anxieties to life again . . .

8

Cathryn stared at the sheet of notepaper which she had furtively, looking about the room, withdrawn from its hiding-place. She knew that she was a fool to keep the letter — that she should have destroyed it the moment she had it in her hands again after Randall had found it in her room and affectionately asked her to 'help him out of a hole'. She had given him the money he wanted and taken her letter thankfully. She had never been sure if he had taken a copy and would one day ask her again for money on the strength of it. Now, with the knowledge that Randall had married that girl in the room along the corridor, there was fear in her eyes that there had been a copy, that it was in Sara's possession and that she might not hesitate to use it. It was a faint hope that Sara might not realise how damaging the letter could be to the man who had written it . . . married to Randall, she must have known his weakness, might have aided and abetted him, might know the many secrets that he had been paid to keep to himself. For Cathryn had known of Randall's tendencies for years and loved him despite the cold, calculating streak in his makeup. She had continued to love him even when she was most horrified by the discovery that he would not hesitate to blackmail his own sister if the opportunity arose. She had loved him and excused him again and again. He was weak, extravagant, loved to exercise a certain power over others, had been spoiled and loved too much all his life. Was it really his fault that, having once discovered that people would pay to keep their secrets from being publicised, he had found a certain excitement in delving into the lives of those he met, discovering things they did not want known and making use of his knowledge to the best advantage? Not always for money — to ensure that certain strings were pulled, to ensure the conquest of a reluctant woman, to ensure an introduction or an invitation . . .

Slowly, she read the damaging letter and tears sprang to her eyes. It was a year since they had met and loved and been forced to part by circumstances but her love was as strong and fierce as ever — and she knew that if fate decreed that Sara knew of the existence of this letter and demanded money for her silence that she would pay and go on paying to protect the man she loved. One day they would be together, their enforced patience knowing its reward, but not if anything was allowed to threaten his brilliant career or the security of his children. His wife had been an invalid for years, tied to a wheelchair — and one day he would be free to take another wife without fear of scandal. Meanwhile, Cathryn cherished the one and only letter that she had ever received from him and knew that their love would eventually surmount all the obstacles . . .

Kyre sensed the wariness, the uneasiness in the house of the last few days and was puzzled. There was a tension, a distrust, a caution in each one's attitude to the other — yet he could not put the finger on the cause. Any mention of Sara caused one to glance instinctively at the other or brought a swift withdrawal to previously frank and fearless eyes — and a visit by one or other of them to Sara's room was greeted with something that was oddly like suspicion and fear.

He did not understand. They seemed to resent and fear the newcomer yet they were eager to ply the most-recent visitor to her room with questions as to her health, her state of mind, their conversation.

It struck him forcibly that Randall's name was studiously avoided. Since his death, they had not mulled over the tragedy more than was natural at the time. They had come to speak of him easily among themselves and at times it almost seemed as though he was merely enjoying himself in London and might well arrive unexpectedly any day. But now they did not speak of him. If Kyre mentioned his name, however casually, the subject was changed — not hastily but noticeably.

He wondered if Sara's presence was a too-constant reminder that Randall was dead, that he would never again walk into a room as easily as though he had not been away from the house, a careless joke on his lips and a warm, teasing smile in his eyes. He had been deeply and sincerely mourned by the family. They had come to terms with their grief but perhaps it was renewed by the knowledge that he had died so soon after his surprising marriage and that a child who bore an amazing likeness to him lay in his cot in the room above.

He was puzzled by the hostility they felt towards Sara. Having loved Randall so much, he had expected them to embrace his widow with affection once her identity was known. He could not complain that she lacked their attentions for all of them had spent some time with Sara during the last few days. She was rarely alone for long. Their natural courtesy and consideration and kindliness seemed to be the answer — yet he could not help feeling that something more lay behind their visits.

Uncle James insisted too frequently that the girl was an impostor and a liar despite all the evidence to the contrary — and it seemed to Kyre that the old man with all his bluster was afraid to accept the truth.

Aunt Dimity said very little but he surprised her more than once with sad eyes and a more pronounced vagueness in her manner betrayed that she was worried and upset — and Kyre, remembering her swift compassion for the girl when she first arrived, wondered that she was so often silent now when the rest of the family spoke of Sara disparagingly.

Philip was edgy and short-tempered

and claimed that he could not work while the house was experiencing so much unrest. He seemed to be forever glancing over his shoulder or moving closer to Melanie as though he needed the comfort of her protection. Kyre liked his brother-in-law and believed that his artistic gift would bring him fame and success one day — but it had always surprised him that his sister had chosen to marry a man who lacked strength of character and purpose. At times, Melanic seemed more mother than wife to the man who cared little for his appearance, was indifferent to food or sleep when inspiration seized him and seldom gave any thought to what the morrow might bring. Now, more than ever, it seemed that Melanie was needed to comfort and soothe and protect him — and there was a tautness and strain about his sister that worried Kyre and made him long to question her. But they had always battled with their own problems and prying into each other's affairs had never been a

Hamilton pastime. Randall had inherited his strong streak of curiosity from his mother — but it had never occurred to Kyre that the boy used his discoveries to advantage.

Kane was sullen and taciturn. He came near to quarrelling with Honor one evening — and she too was roused to bitter retort and flushed cheeks. Usually so calm and composed, so self-possessed, her annoyance and discomposure were very obvious. Kyre knew that his twin was half in love with Honor and he wished that Kane would do something about it. Surely he did not imagine that he would be poaching on his brother's preserves? It must be obvious to everyone, including Honor, by this time that he was not a marrying man! He was not a proud man himself therefore he did not realise that his twin was too proud to ask any woman to marry him while he was without the money to support her without assistance. Nor was he a suspicious man and he had gladly handed over the estate accounts to his twin and rarely bothered to check the figures — or he might have wondered long since why machinery was so often replaced or that it needed so many men to run the home farm or that they were so unlucky with their stock . . .

Of them all, Cathryn seemed untouched by the general unrest. Her gaiety and vivacity were much in evidence and she managed to even the balance between normality and a rare despondency. When she had chaffed Kane and Honor out of their disagreement, brought the smile back to Aunt Dimity's eyes, restored Uncle James to his usual good humour and eased the edginess from Philip and the motherliness from Melanie with a lively game of cards, Kyre was able to tell himself that he had imagined everything and laugh at his fears and fancies. Relaxing with his pipe, he forgot to wonder at Cathryn's slightly unnatural gaiety . . . forgot that she was most vivacious when she was unhappy and chose to conceal it . . .

Sara did not particularly welcome the visits that each of the family made from time to time but they were a relief from the boredom which possessed her. She hated the enforced inactivity and longed to be away from the house which seemed to stifle her with its atmosphere of tradition and family and fierce loyalties. She did not think that Kyre Hamilton or anyone else would attempt to discourage her from leaving. She did not feel like a member of the family. She had not been accepted by any of them. She did not fit in with their unhurried, calmly accepting lives. As soon as she was well enough to work, she would take any part that was offered — and if Kyre were to suggest that she should have the allowance which had come to an end on Randall's death, then she would accept it gratefully for Adam's sake. If not — she would manage in some way to provide for him, to educate him — despite her original intention, she would not leave him with the

Hamiltons, she thought with a fierce surge of love and tenderness. Come what may, she was determined that he should grow up in a different atmosphere to the one that had formed Randall's character!

Sitting in a comfortable chair by the blazing fire, the cot by her side and an unopened magazine in her lap, Sara thought about her visitors. They were always pleasant, solicitous, friendly — yet something in their manner did not accord with their conversation. Analysis evaded her and she was puzzled.

Aunt Dimity had been the first to arouse her suspicions. Sara was convinced that the old lady had been either trying to tell her something — or to find out something. Her gentle voice had held anxiety, her faded blue eyes had been keen and shrewd and there had been a strange determination in her bearing.

Uncle James had stomped into the room with a purposeful air and a smile that just failed to be benevolent and kindly.

'Well, young lady — how are you feeling now, eh? Is this the cause of all the upset?' He had bent over the cot, making ridiculous cluckings and snapping his fingers at the sleeping baby. 'A fine boy, my dear — just like his father. Yes, indeed, the image of poor Randall.' He had turned to look at her and, meeting a faint amusement in her gaze, hurrumped and strode away from the cot, a dull brick colour suffusing his face. 'Thought I'd better come and pay my respects to you and the boy. I'm James Hamilton, Randall's uncle. I expect he told you about me, eh?'

She had looked at him steadily. 'Many times.'

He had looked up quickly at her reply. 'Hm! Did he? Disrespectful young man — I expect he told you I was a blithering old fool, eh?' He had laughed indulgently but she felt that he was waiting for her reply with some anxiety.

Words had echoed in her brain, words

spoken in that laughing, scathing tone: *'The old fool is a frightful bore. You'd need to be pretty green to believe half of his tall stories. If you believe him, he's left a trail of glory half across the world. More likely a trail of seduced women and howling brats! For all his adventures, he hasn't a penny to bless himself with — and his only legacy is a lame leg. He has a different version about that leg every time — a crocodile took a fancy to Hamilton meat in Darkest Africa — a desperate rogue took an axe to him in Cape Town — a horse trampled on him when he was helping to quell a riot in New South Wales. I think the old fool even believes his taraddidles himself . . . but it's my guess the truth would make pretty hearing!'*

As always, when speaking of any member of his family except Kyre, there had been that secretive, mocking light in his eyes — a look that she had come to dread for it usually meant that he knew something to the discredit of the person and knew how to use his knowledge.

Not for the first time, Sara wondered if he had lived so well not only by the generosity of his cousin but also by the proceeds of a certain knowledge about members of his family. He had admired and respected Kyre . . . that was evident even while he mocked his cousin's obsession with family ties and family loyalties and derided him for his lack of vices and scorned him as a man who didn't know he was alive. Having met Kyre and felt the strength of character, sensed integrity and honesty and compassion in his make-up, knowing a reluctant admiration and respect for him herself, Sara could believe him to be the only man that Randall had feared and wanted to impress and whose approval and affection he sought — and she thought it unlikely that he had been one of Randall's victims.

But she could not be so certain where the others were concerned . . .

She said tactfully: 'I think Randall was very fond of you.'

Relief touched the old man's eyes.

Straightening his back, he had patted the crisp hair hair at his temples. 'Yes . . . we were always good friends. He's very much missed, you know — but it was very remiss of him to get married without a word to anyone. All very sudden, eh?'

'Yes, it was . . . sudden,' she said in a tone that did not brook any further questions.

He nodded. 'Impetuous as always — had to have whatever he wanted almost before he knew he wanted it. One had to admire his stick-at-nothing ways . . . although he might not always have been too scrupulous about the means to an end.' He had sent her a sharp, shrewd glance.

Sara had known then that he was afraid — but not the reason for his fear. 'It doesn't always pay to have scruples,' she had replied thoughtlessly.

The colour had deepened in his face. Muttering that he must not tire her, that he had things to do, he had hastily escaped from the room — and Sara had cursed her careless tongue for frightening him away before he had said something which might have cleared up the mystery.

Kane's visit had been brief, almost punctilious as though he offered courtesy to a guest only at his brother's instigation. Sara had been startled by his likeness to Kyre but later, alone again, she had time to realise that it was no more than a superficial resemblance — that the two men were in fact poles apart in type and character. She had not liked Kane with his lazy drawl and the hint of frightening strength in his indolent movements and the keen penetration of his dark eyes. His visit had been an enigma . . .

He had burst abruptly into the room almost immediately after Carol had left it — as though he had been waiting for an opportunity to find her alone.

He had looked at her for a long moment and then grinned. That smile had irritated her unreasonably — perhaps it was the sudden reminder of

Randall's swift assessment of a woman and the realisation that this man was amused and curious about his cousin's choice of a wife. She had known instinctively that this must be Kane Hamilton: . . . '*a bit of a brute and not to be trusted with women or money. I suppose he's a good farmer but if I ever come into money remind me never to let Kane have the handling of it — he'd feather his own nest and show me a handful of plausible accounts to allay suspicion. He's been making love to his brother's woman behind Kyre's back for years — I hope to be around when Kyre gets to know about it...*' Sara had attached little importance to those light-hearted remarks, thinking only that Randall's contempt of his cousin was nevertheless touched with a certain admiration. Studying the tall, broad-shouldered, powerful Kane as he stood by the door of her room, she could recognise the sensuality, the passionate brutality, the fire and the ice in the dark gleam of his eyes and the half-sneering, half-smiling curve of his lips.

His scrutiny embarrassed and annoyed her. 'Well?'

'You're not what I'd expected,' he had said bluntly.

'Should I apologise?' Her voice had been cold, angry.

'Did I say that I was disappointed?' His parry was quick, forceful.

'It was implied.'

He had laughed gently. 'Maybe I'm relieved,' he had pointed out.

'Why?'

Thrusting his hands into his pockets, he had lounged carelessly against the door. 'Because the mice are scurrying into their holes — and the cat turns out to be a meek little kitten with a piece of cheese that she doesn't know what to do with.'

'I don't understand you.'

'I wonder? Oh, don't flash those innocent eyes at me, pussy — you know why the mice are scared but I don't think you mean them any harm. Or do you? I could be wrong about you, of course.'

She had stared at him. Then, slowly: 'You're Kane, aren't you?'

He had executed a mock bow. 'None other! Did you recognise me from my cousin's far-from-flattering description — or it is merely guesswork?'

'You resemble Kyre,' she had told him quietly.

'Twins are often alike,' he had mocked her. Then, hearing footsteps in the corridor, he had opened the door and saying carelessly: 'We must have a longer talk next time, sweet cousin,' had gone from the room as abruptly as he had entered it.

His remarks had puzzled her very much. She did not know why he should have been so cryptic, at what he had been hinting throughout their brief conversation, why there had been so much insolence in his mocking voice. But she found herself wondering if he was apprehensive of her unexpected and apparently unwelcome intrusion into the house. She was not a fool and she had swiftly realised that almost every member of the family entered her room with fear as their invisible shadow. Why should they be afraid? She could do them no harm. It could not be resentment of Randall's secret marriage for none of them could have gained anything by his death as a bachelor — or was she wrong? Was it possible that Randall had been Kyre's heir and that as his widow she stood in the way of an inheritance they had expected once Randall was killed? It seemed fantastic, impossible — but it was the only explanation that occurred to her.

Melanie was in and out of the room on various pretexts, bringing books and photographs of her children, offering her services, announcing that she had a few minutes to spare and thought Sara might like some company. Her manner was casual, her conversation light and easy — and Sara told herself firmly that she imagined a wariness, a certain uneasiness, a tendency for Melanie to introduce her husband's name into the coversation. Randall had told her very little about Philip except that he was not as talented as the man believed and would never make a name for himself in the art world, that he was an American but showed a strange reluctance to return to his own country, that he had never been able to fathom Melanie's reasons for marrying such a poor specimen of manhood . . . *'She might have chosen a better man to father her precious infants — she'll only have herself to blame if either of them have inherited the bad seed.'*

It was obvious that Melanie was a loving wife and a doting mother and to Sara it was not difficult to understand why she should have married Philip Kennedy. But there was more than affection in her tone whenever she spoke of her husband, Sara thought shrewdly. There was concern and fear and caution.

Sara was very conscious that she was an outsider. The big house oppressed her and she frequently regretted the promise which had brought her to it in time to have her child beneath its roof. So yet another Hamilton had been born in the house — but of what benefit was that to Adam or to Sara herself? She was impatient to be well enough to leave the house and its strange, hostile, superficially friendly inhabitants. She could not feel that she was a member of the family. She could not feel that any one of them offered a welcome or a sincere friendliness. She could not feel at ease or content — except when she cradled her son in her arms and looked in wonder at his small, perfect face and beautiful hands and sturdy, healthy body. She was ready, indeed willing, to discuss his perfections — but nothing would induce her to discuss her marriage, her brief life with Randall or her own background and family.

She did not like or trust the Hamiltons — except for Kyre who had given her no reason to dislike or distrust him and she saw him very seldom. No doubt he was occupied with his writing, his family affairs, the woman who was generally referred to as 'the girl Kyre means to marry one day' but whose name and personality were unknown to Sara. She was not interested enough to pursue the subject whenever it cropped up during her conversations with Melanie — but she did wonder at the type of woman who could keep one man on a string indefinitely while carrying on an affair with his brother at the same time. Was Kyre really so ignorant of the circumstances — or was it possible that he knew and did not care? Nothing would surprise her where the Hamiltons were concerned, she thought grimly and somewhat contemptuously.

9

She did not realise that her impressions of the family had been biased months before by Randall's slighting comments. When she thought of Uncle James as a boring old fool, of Aunt Dimity as a silly, inconsequential old lady, of Kane as a brutal, sensual man without morals or principles, of Melanie as an anxious hen struggling to keep all her chicks under one wing, of Kyre as a remote, somewhat pompous figurehead, she did not realise that her judgment had been influenced long before she met any of them.

Cathryn was different. Cathryn she liked and welcomed to her room on the occasions when she came to sit and chatter lightly and admire her nephew. She could not know that her impulsive liking for her sister-in-law stemmed from the fact that Randall had seldom mentioned his sister and never criticised or condemned her in her hearing.

She could be at ease with Cathryn. The warmth and gaiety of her personality seemed to bring sunshine into the room that contrasted with the greyness of the outside world — for the weather had not improved during the few days that she had been at Hamilton House.

Cathryn was not enigmatic, wary, probing or tactless. She seemed to accept Sara as her brother's widow without comment or question. She rarely talked about Randall but always with affectionate indulgence that was only slightly tinged with a reminder of her grief. She was willing to talk on any subject under the sun. She seemed interested in Sara's theatrical career and encouraged her to talk about the theatre, about current plays, about famous theatricals she had met or worked with. She did not pry into the circumstances of Sara's meeting with Randall and the reasons for that subsequent, hasty marriage. She seemed to offer genuine friendship, a shy and tentative liking and betrayed a flattering preference for her company.

Her likeness to Randall was marked — but she showed no signs of his weakness, his vicious enjoyment of power, his sensuality and slyness, his curiosity and mercenary outlook. Sara thought of her as a young, lively, happy girl with plenty of menfriends, an active social life and the natural ambitions of any young girl for eventual marriage, a home of her own and children . . .

'You seem to spend a lot of time in Sara's room,' Kyre remarked carelessly. 'How do you get on with her?'

'Well enough. But I do wonder what on earth Randall saw in her, Kyre. She just isn't his type.'

He smiled. 'What was his type, darling?'

'Oh, I don't know . . . glamour, sophistication. The type to play his own game of dangerous flirtation and accept his eventual wearying of it without a scene. Sara isn't that type at all.'

'Perhaps because it wasn't a dangerous flirtation but marriage he had in mind,' he said shrewdly. 'A man doesn't usually marry the type of woman he flirts with, you know.'

'I suppose he was in love with her,' Cathryn said doubtfully, taking a cigarette from the offered box.

'Does it seem so unlikely?' He provided her with a light and smiled down at the lovely face with its troubled expression.

'He might have wanted to hop into bed with a girl like Sara — but I just can't believe that he would marry her,' she said bluntly.

He raised an eyebrow. 'Why do you say that?'

'Oh, she's too quiet, too introspective, too dull. She'd have bored Randall to death in a year!'

'Oh, come! Isn't that a little sweeping?' he challenged lightly. 'You scarcely know Sara — and appearances can be deceptive. Frankly, I wouldn't think of her as boring — quiet and reserved, a little on the defensive, straight-forward and not afraid to speak her mind — but not boring.'

She wrinkled her nose at him. 'That's exactly what I mean!' she exclaimed cryptically. He looked an enquiry. 'Well . . . that kind of girl might suit you down to the ground,' she went on. 'But never Randall!' Her tone was very emphatic.

He smiled. 'Perhaps we were not so different at heart as you think, Cathryn.' He did not contend the startling statement that Sara or a girl like her would make him a suitable wife — an omission that Cathryn noticed but scarcely heeded. 'I imagine Sara appealed to Randall in a way that you cannot understand. Perhaps because she is so different to the women he had known.'

'Well, she's secretive and that's what I don't like about her,' Cathryn blurted impulsively.

'Secretive? Is she? In what way?'

Faint colour rose in her cheeks. 'Oh, I

don't mean that she isn't forthcoming if you ask questions — but there's something about her that forestalls questions. And I do hate the way she looks sometimes — as though she knows something but isn't prepared to admit it . . . as though she can see right through me and isn't impressed!'

Kyre laughed easily. 'Darling, you seem quite upset — what on earth can she know about you other than what Randall might have told her?'

'Well, that's it,' she muttered beneath her breath.

Kyre went on carelessly: 'I think you misinterpret a very natural shyness and a somewhat defensive manner. We are all strangers — and she is in an unenviable position. I think she may have sensed our suspicion and distrust when she first came and she can't be blamed for attributing any sudden friendliness to vulgar curiosity.'

'Does she indeed?' Cathryn asked swiftly, coldly.

He laughed. 'I haven't the faintest

idea, darling. I really haven't discussed it with her.'

She looked at him thoughtfully. 'No . . . you haven't seen very much of her at all, have you, Kyre?'

He was vaguely disturbed by something in her voice and manner that he could not define. 'No . . . why?'

She rose and stubbed her cigarette in a convenient ashtray. 'Oh . . . no reason,' she said carelessly. 'I'm just a little surprised at your eagerness to take up the cudgels on her behalf when you hardly know her — and don't seem very interested in knowing her any better.'

'I've been busy,' he said defensively, as though she accused him of neglecting his guest. 'I'll meet her often enough when she's well enough to leave her room.'

'She's going back to London,' she said, walking towards the door.

'Is she? Has she told you so?' He was conscious of a strange disappointment.

'Did you think she would stay here?'

'I've told her to think of the place as her home.'

'But . . . didn't it occur to you that we might not want her here?' she asked hotly.

Kyre stiffened. 'Is that the general feeling?' He was oddly irritated by the family's hostility to Sara.

'Surely it's obvious? She doesn't belong here, Kyre — she's an outsider. She would never fit in — and you must be the only one to think of encouraging her to stay with us.'

'Then it isn't surprising that she's so determined to go back to London,' he said grimly and turned away to stare into the fire, his back conveying his displeasure and disappointment.

Cathryn looked at him dispassionately for a long moment. Dear Kyre . . . always so quick to help a lame dog over a stile, to smooth the way for others, to iron out a disagreement. Always so concerned with the family, so reluctant to lose any one of them, so eager to offer a welcome to any new member of the family. She was sure that Philip's conscience never pricked him that he was content to live in another man's house, to eat the food that was provided and paid for by another man, to know that his wife and children benefited by the generosity of another man, to spend his days with palette and paints, easel and canvas without concerning himself about the future. Now it seemed that Kyre was equally as willing to do as much for Sara as he had already done for Philip . . . provide her and her son with a home, feed and clothe her, draw her into the small and intimate family group until she would eventually become an integral part of it. Not because he liked her . . . he hardly knew her . . . but because she had married a Hamilton! The fact that she had determined to have her child beneath the roof of Hamilton House must have endeared her to Kyre, too!

With a tiny shrug of her slim shoulders, she went from the room . . .

Kyre thought over his conversation

with Cathryn . . . and decided that her remark *had* been a reprimand for the neglect of his guest. It was true that he had neglected Sara. He had been reluctant to visit her again and eased his conscience with the reminder that she did not lack for company and that she would scarcely expect him to be for ever visiting her bedroom.

He wished he could dislike Sara and be done with it. But he did not dislike her. Indeed, he admired and respected her. He thought that she had courage and spirit and a certain independence. He thought that she was honest and sincere . . . as true as steel. He smiled as the hackneyed phrase leaped to his mind.

Odd, he thought, I hardly know her — yet I feel as though I've always known her. Cathryn is wrong . . . Sara does belong, she does fit in, this house welcomed her and so did I — as though we were both waiting for her all these years.

Abruptly, almost guiltily, he hurried

the thought from his mind. It was not like him to indulge in such fancies . . . and he drew his chair closer to the fire and reached out a hand for his pipe and pouch.

For at least ten minutes he strove to think of other things . . . and for at least ten minutes he was successful. Then, insidiously but forcefully, denying to be denied, the thought of Sara crept back into his mind as he drowsed by the blazing fire . . .

He could understand Cathryn's bewilderment — the obvious surprise that all the family shared. No one would have expected Randall to show so much good taste, so much common sense in choosing a wife. His taste in women had always been towards the extravagant, the glamorous, the sophisticated, the flippant and the temporary. But Sara was none of these things. She was small and neat and sensitive, reserved and perhaps a little shy. Her only claims to beauty lay in the rarity of her pale blonde hair and those candid, straightforward, lovely grey eyes. She was not sophisticated: she was too direct, too blunt, too outspoken, too untouched by the world in which she had presumably moved as a member of the theatrical profession. He could not imagine her as a dissembler. She might not always be tactful or pleasant but she would always be honest. Her very difference to those other women in Randall's life must explain her attraction for him — and Kyre thought that his cousin had chosen wisely. Unfortunate that there had not been time enough for him to settle down, to enjoy the advantages of marriage to a woman like Sara, to realise the advantage of pure gold, over dross, to appreciate the rarity of his wife's character and qualities.

He could understand why Randall had chosen Sara. But why had she married him? He had been attractive, charming, well-mannered, even-tempered and lovable — but never by word nor expression had she betrayed any love for her husband. Rather the reverse, Kyre thought ruefully — and wondered.

Did she have an unsuspected mercenary streak? Had she believed Randall to be wealthy, influential, an asset to an unknown and ambitious actress? Or had she impulsively fallen in love and rushed into marriage only to realise too late that her love had been no more than infatuation, that she had nothing in common with the man she had married, that they were both condemned to a mockery of marriage — and had she illogically blamed Randall for the haste of that marriage and for the conception of the child she had admitted that she did not want? Had nothing been left of her former affection for Randall but the foul taste of mistake in her mouth?

Kyre did not know and knew he could never ask for the answers to these questions. One day, perhaps, when they were friends and she had grown to trust him, she would tell him the circumstances of her marriage. But it would not matter if he never knew — for he realised now that nothing she might have done in the past could alter the undeniable feeling that she had awakened in him.

Her pale, oval face with its sensitive mouth and determined chin and luminous eyes seemed to haunt him. So did her cool, self-possessed yet enchanting voice, echoing again and again in his thoughts.

He was frank with himself now, admitting the reason for his recent neglect of Sara. It was unthinkable that he should have fallen abruptly and somewhat immaturely in love with a woman he scarcely knew — and that woman the widow of his cousin! He had kept away from her room with a determination to thrust such fancies out of his mind and heart. But he had not succeeded. This was the one woman to bring dormant passion to life, to destroy the belief that he was incapable of loving any woman, to dismiss for ever the half-formed resolution of marrying

Honor eventually.

He felt that Sara had been badly hurt, lonely and unhappy and anxious — all his protective instincts were aroused but it was not only her need of his strength and compassion and tenderness that stirred him to love for the first time in his life. He was angered anew that Randall had left them all in ignorance of his surprise marriage. So much heartache, bitterness and loneliness could have been avoided if he had known of Sara's existence when Randall died.

But he could make amends now. He would dissuade her from leaving his house and if it led to disagreements among the family . . . well, that was unfortunate but easily overcome. Sara and her child were his responsibilities now and he was prepared to shoulder them willingly. He did not consciously visualise a future with Sara as his wife — but he knew that he loved her deeply and felt that she must recognise in time that their happiness in life depended on each other.

His family did not like Sara but they would accept her eventually. He felt that she had not set herself out to be liked. Her blunt speaking and cold reserve and antagonistic manner did not augur for popularity — but in time she would soften and accept the family as her own. Her life with Randall had evidently been unhappy . . . one could not expect her to look kindly on his family or to believe at first that his family did not share the faults and characteristics that she had disliked and resented in her husband.

Kyre knocked ash from his pipe and rose to his feet, pushing his spaniel's head from his knee. Cathryn had been right to remind him that Sara must notice his neglect. Now was as good a time as any to rectify the fault . . .

As he left his study, the main door opened on a cold gust of air and laughing, well-known voices gave him pause. He turned to smile a greeting.

Honor neatly extricated herself from the vice-like arm about her waist and came forward, smiling and composed, smoothing the dark hair that had been tossed by the wind. Her glowing cheeks and bright eyes conveyed a picture of health. In her expensive, well-cut riding habit, she was slim, elegant and very beautiful. It struck Kyre forcibly that she was as dark and purposeful as Sara was fair and anchorless.

'It's a beastly day!' she exclaimed vibrantly. 'Sensible of you not to venture out, Kyre.'

Kane followed her, tall, imperturbable, a faint smile of mockery in the depths of his dark eyes. He nodded briefly to his brother.

'Enjoy your ride?' Kyre asked courteously.

'We didn't go far. Kane insisted on showing me the new barns,' she went on lightly. 'He just won't believe that I'm not a countrywoman at heart.'

Smiling, Kyre retrieved a haystraw from her dark hair. 'You made a thorough inspection,' he said carelessly.

For the briefest of moments, she was at a loss. Then she said smoothly: 'Oh, that brother of yours is a child at heart. He said I only needed a straw in my hair to look the true yokel — I'd forgotten about it.'

'Let's have a drink,' Kane said abruptly, moving towards the sitting-room. 'What will you have — cider?'

Honor laughed. 'See what I mean? No, I'll have sherry. Come and have a drink with us, Kyre?'

He hesitated. Then realised that a few minutes made little difference to his plans. 'Yes, of course.'

He accepted a drink and smiled dutifully and replied absently as they tried to draw him into their bantering exchange. But he was thinking with some astonishment that he had been amazingly obtuse until this moment. There was more of the approach of lovers than friends in their easy banter, their exchange of warm, laughing, almost secretive glances, the seemingly natural blending of one personality with the other. Quite dispassionately he realised that they were lovers and knew his twin too well not to recognise the look of triumphant satisfaction — and he was mature enough to recognise the evidence of lovemaking in the warm softness of her mouth and the brightness of her eyes and the radiance of her mood. But he disliked the thought that they deemed it necessary to carry on a furtive affair. Honor was not a village girl to be tumbled in the hay — but it was a proof of Kane's approach that he should choose to do just that. No doubt he enjoyed humbling the arrogance and disturbing the cool self-possession that characterised Honor so much.

He was unaware of a certain coolness in his manner towards them — but when he had left them, Honor turned to Kane with anger in her eyes. 'You fool! I'm sure he suspects!'

'So? Is that such a tragedy?' He smiled mockingly. 'I admire your quick thinking, my sweet — straws in your hair, indeed! Did you really expect him to believe you?'

'You really are a devil,' she said,

half-admiringly. 'Have you no con-science?'

He shrugged. 'You're not married to Kyre.'

'Not yet,' she replied tautly.

'I hate to shatter your illusions but Kyre will never marry you,' he said decisively.

The heat of anger burned in her cheeks. 'I'm determined that he will!'

His own temper flared abruptly. 'So to salve your wretched pride and satisfy your mercenary little heart, you'll manoeuvre him into it and to hell with *my* feelings!'

'Oh, don't be a fool,' she said coldly. 'You're not capable of real feeling. You only want one thing of me — so cut out the dramatics!'

His eyes narrowed to flints of contemptuous steel. But only briefly. Then his gaze was warm and mocking. 'Of course. I might propose in the heat of the moment — but I'd run like a hare if you took me up on it. You serve well enough for a mistress but I'm damned if

I'd wed a woman like you. You're not the type that men marry, Honor — except highly principled men like my dear brother. Snap him up if you can. You may never meet another like him — there are more like me in this world!' He chose his words with deliberate care, seeking to hurt, knowing that she was more vulnerable than she cared to admit to the world in general.

She stared at him, the colour draining from her face at the deliberate insult of his words. She could not believe that this was the same man who had held her close, kissed her lips, her eyes, her hair, her throat, the gleaming paleness of her body with tenderness rather than passion, murmured of his love and begged her to marry him and urged her to the final surrender with sweetness and warmth and gentle loving. This man looked at her with a hateful, contemptuous mockery, spurned the memory of their recent lovemaking, tossed the gift she had withheld for so long back in her face and taunted her as though she were an easy conquest for any man. Pain and humiliation swept through her entire being — and she wished with all her heart that she had held out against his entreaties and the sweet deceit of his tender, loving words.

He continued to smile and his eyes continued to mock her with their warm amusement at her discomfiture and humiliation.

'You're . . . detestable,' she said unevenly, her voice breaking slightly.

'Are we to part like this?' he bantered, tilting her chin with a none-too-gentle hand.

She wrenched away from his touch. 'I . . . think — I hate you!' she said in low tones.

'Do you?' He laughed softly. 'Well, that's an improvement on your former indifference.' He picked up her empty glass. 'Another sherry?'

'No!'

'You won't join me? Pity.' He turned to smile as he poured the amber liquid into his own glass. 'I suppose you're wishing that you had a phial of poison to hand.'

She made no reply, turning violently towards the fire, holding her cold hands to the blaze. She was suddenly completely chilled.

He came over to stand behind her and abruptly he stooped to touch the nape of her neck with his lips. A sudden tremor ran through her body and she jerked away furiously.

His eyes held mischief as he said lightly: 'We must visit the barn again. Perhaps we can improve on your hate of me, my sweet.'

She sent him a look so full of revulsion, of loathing, of contempt not only for him but for herself that he sobered immediately.

'No need to hate me quite so violently,' he said quietly. 'You knew I didn't mean it, Honor. I was trying to hurt you — as much as you've hurt me. Isn't it your turn to cut out the dramatics?'

She slapped his face.

As the door closed behind her, Kane threw his sherry glass against the fireplace with the savage force of fury — and knew that his hopes of marrying Honor were now as shattered as that once-lovely glass . . .

10

Kyre mounted the wide staircase slowly. He told himself that he had never played fair with Honor. He had allowed her to believe that one day he would marry her — and she had believed it for too long. He could not blame her for turning to Kane for the fire and passion that she had failed to stir in him. Neither did he blame Kane for taking advantage of her brief interest in him. He should have realised long since the way the wind was blowing — and made it clear to Honor that his affection for her could never lead to marriage. She should marry Kane — but were his emotions so deeply involved? Kyre could not imagine his twin with a wife — neither could he imagine Kane's interest in any woman lasting for long once the conquest was achieved. But he could be wrong . . .

He knocked lightly on the door of Sara's room and heard her clear voice bid him enter.

She made no attempt to hide her surprise. He smiled a little self-consciously. 'You're looking very well.'

'I am well.'

He nodded. 'Well enough to come down to dinner, do you think?'

'I'd rather not,' she said bluntly.

He drew up a chair and sat down, leaning forward to touch the tiny hand of her son as he nestled in her lap. 'I'm rather surprised to find you alone,' he said lightly, deciding to ignore her direct reply to his question. 'I thought you were besieged by visitors.'

'I have been — but I expect the novelty is wearing off. They are all very curious about me, you know — but I'm afraid I haven't been very forthcoming.'

'Why should you be?' he agreed, smiling at the child. 'I think it's the first time I've known him to be really awake,' he commented. 'He seems fascinated by the fire.'

She looked down at her son with the look in her eyes that he had seen in Melanie's when her babies were small and helpless. 'His eyes can't focus yet,' she told him.

'I hear that you've named him Adam.'

She nodded. 'It isn't a family name. Do you mind?' Her tone implied that any objection on his part would mean nothing to her.

'Of course not. He's your baby,' he said in surprise. 'I rather like the name.' He smiled at her gently. 'I didn't expect you to choose a family name, Sara.'

Her glance was swift, perceptive. 'Is it so obvious?'

'That you haven't much time for Hamiltons? It is to me. I don't know if the others realise it.'

For the first time, she seemed a little embarrassed. That direct gaze was turned towards the leaping flames of the fire. He studied the small, neat profile — and wondered that he had originally thought her to be without beauty. Her features were delicately-etched and the purity of the bone formation hinted that she would be lovely when the years had taken the bloom of youth.

'I expect so,' she said quietly. 'I haven't been very friendly, you know.' She looked up with a sudden, almost mischievous smile. 'I'm not a very comfortable guest, am I?'

'I don't think of you as a guest,' he replied evenly.

'But I am — and a very transitory one,' she said firmly. 'Dr. Marsden assures me that I shall be quite well enough to travel within a few days and I've already made my plans.'

'May I know them?'

She gave a tiny shrug. 'Saval is producing a new play. I've worked for him before and he might be persuaded to give me a part. If not, I shall try television — commercials and small parts, I expect.' She added frankly: 'I'll never be a star, I know — I'm not the type. But I enjoy the work and I'm not much good at anything else. I have an attractive voice and a certain presence — as one of the critics was pleased to note in his column. I've been in the business since I was eighteen and never been forced to 'rest' until Adam was on the way.'

'Where will you live?'

'I'll find a flat,' she said confidently.

'I believe that isn't too easy these days.'

'I know a girl who will let me share her place until I find something.'

He was silent for a moment. Then he asked gently: 'And the boy? Do your plans include him?'

Instinctively her arms tightened around her son. 'Of course.'

He noted the swift, proud tilting of her chin. 'Then you've changed your mind during the last few days.'

'Circumstances have changed,' she pointed out decisively. 'For one thing, I didn't think I was the maternal type . . . for another, I believed that Randall was alive and could be landed with the responsibility for his child.'

'You could still leave him with us,' he

said tentatively. 'Carol is very efficient and Melanie will be only too pleased to take him under her wing. He will still be your child, of course — and you are perfectly free to come and go as you please.'

She shook her head. 'No, Kyre.'

He smiled at her gently. 'Still on the defensive? I'm not trying to part you from your child, Sara. But you seem to have made up your mind to leave this house — and you were the one to declare that there isn't any place for a child in the theatre. Do you mean to bring him up in a dressing-room?'

Her mouth set in stubborn lines. 'I'm not leaving him, Kyre.' She went on abruptly: 'Why should I consign him to the care of Carol and Melanie? A child needs its mother!'

'I agree,' he said smoothly. 'You should stay here and look after him yourself. Does the theatre really mean so much to you?'

'I wouldn't be happy here,' she said, almost fiercely.

'I'm sorry you feel like that. But isn't Adam's happiness of more importance? Would it be a satisfactory way of life for him? Would you always have enough time to devote to him? Would he grow up in the right atmosphere? With a true sense of values?'

She flashed him a swift, angry glance. 'Meaning that I'm being selfish? Perhaps you're right. But this isn't exactly the ideal atmosphere for a child, is it?'

He raised an eyebrow. 'Quite a few children have grown up in this house, you know. And it doesn't seem to have done them any harm.'

'What about Randall?' she asked bitterly.

'Randall? Yes, he grew up here,' he said, puzzled. After a momentary hesitation, he went on: 'You apparently knew a side to Randall that this family neither knew nor suspected. Do you blame this house because your marriage was unsatisfactory?' Surprise and bewilderment were evident in his voice.

'Not the house . . . the environment, the relationships, the lack of perception and the people who live here,' she said bluntly.

'I see,' he said, completely at a loss.

She laughed tautly. 'Of course you don't! Just like the others, you thought Randall was perfect. And, like the others, you wonder why on earth he married me, don't you?'

Kyre smiled at her warmly. 'No, I don't,' he said in all sincerity. 'I think he must have been very much in love with you, Sara.'

Taken aback, she stared at him. She could not doubt that he meant his words — and she flushed a little, not so naïve that she did not realise the compliment behind them. But she said stiffly: 'Well, you're wrong. Randall never loved anyone but himself in his life.' He looked at her steadily and she went on bluntly: 'He wanted to go to bed with me and marriage was the only way!'

'I see,' he said again.

She recognised the faint embarrassment, the compassion that was so misplaced, the sympathy and tenderness for the bitterness he imagined that she felt. She studied him with a sudden, unexpected warmth of feeling. Of all the Hamiltons, he was certainly the only one she could like and trust — and in that moment she felt oddly close to him. Involuntarily she placed her hand over his strong, brown fingers and smiled at the look of surprise in his eyes.

'I think he believed himself in love with me at first,' she said quietly. 'A man like Randall would fall in love with the apparently unattainable — and he knew that I wasn't interested in him.'

'Yet . . . ' He broke off, stemming the question that had leaped to his lips. He had determined never to question her and he would not do so.

'Yet I married him?' she finished for him. 'Yes. I had no choice in the matter,' she added grimly.

'I wish I understood,' he said helplessly.

She looked at him with her head tilted slightly to one side, a faint smile playing about her lips. 'You really didn't know Randall very well, did you?'

'I'm beginning to think so,' he agreed. 'Or else you were never married to my cousin but to another man by the same name!'

'No . . . he told me too much about you all for that,' she said decisively. She hesitated, wondering if she could really trust him with the truth, wondering if he would believe her story if she did — yet feeling that she must justify her action in marrying a man she neither liked nor loved. 'It's a long story,' she said slowly.

He nodded. 'You don't have to tell me, Sara. I accept that you had your reasons — and it's all in the past now, isn't it?'

Again that faintly mischievous smile touched her eyes. 'But isn't that your hobby . . . past history, I mean?' She added impulsively: 'I'd like to tell you, Kyre . . . I think *you* will understand.'

216

So he listened in silence while she unfolded the story . . . a strange story which he found difficult to credit but could not doubt because the light of honesty shone in her eyes and because her quiet voice never faltered once during its telling . . .

Her mother had been ill for years with cancer — an illness that slowly but inexorably took its toll and could lead to only one final ending. She had never been without pain and the last year of her life had been spent as a helpless cripple. Quietly, briefly, Sara conveyed the impressionable, vulnerable girl with a hatred of suffering who had been forced to watch her mother's agonies and know herself helpless to ease them. She told dispassionately of the months of nursing, the long nights of vigil, the burdens thrust on a sixteen year old girl and of the many times that her mother had pleaded with her to increase the number of sleeping tablets that it was Sara's task to administer at night. Time and again she had resisted and seen the reproach and the plea in her mother's eyes. It was inevitable that the young girl, distressed, uncertain, bewildered, should finally give way and she had dropped the extra tablets into the glass of water with trembling hands and a fearful heart . . . the tablets that had ensured the freedom from the travesty of her life that her mother craved. She had died peacefully in her sleep — and Sara had been completely unable to conjure up a sense of guilt.

She paused at this point and glanced uncertainly at Kyre, half-expecting to read condemnation in his eyes, to sense a shrinking from a self-confessed murderess, an abrupt coolness in his usually warm and kindly manner.

He smiled — a gentle, compassionate smile that touched her heart. 'Go on,' he said quietly.

'I didn't think anyone would ever know. The doctor signed the death certificate . . . he didn't seem at all suspicious. He told us that it was a merciful release, that Mother's heart couldn't have taken any more suffering . . . '

'Us? I'm sorry . . . I didn't mean to interrupt you,' he added quickly.

'My brother and I,' she explained briefly. 'He was down from Oxford at the time.' She was silent for a moment then she mustered her courage and went on: 'I was horrified to learn that Simon knew what I'd done . . . he was coming to say goodnight to Mother and saw how many tablets I dropped into the water. I think it was then that I realised exactly what I had done — the enormity of it, I mean. And yet it hadn't seemed wrong . . . I still don't think it was wrong,' she said vehemently.

'Your brother accused you?'

'Oh, it wasn't like that. He understood. He loved Mother, too — he said he was glad, that he'd often wished he had the courage to be merciful.'

Kyre nodded silently. It had taken courage, he thought — or had it been the action of a distressed girl, scarcely conscious of what she was doing? He didn't think so, recalling the quiet intensity of her account.

'I knew Simon wouldn't breathe a word to anyone. Why should he? We only had each other,' she said simply. 'He went back to Oxford after the funeral and on my seventeenth birthday, a month later, I went to London. I'd always wanted to act and the money that Mother left paid for a two year course with RADA. Simon got his degree and took a job abroad and I got my first part in a touring play about the same time.' She glanced at him shrewdly. 'Please don't think that I wanted my mother's death, Kyre — not for myself. I wasn't unhappy at home . . . I wasn't impatient to lead my own life. I just couldn't bear to see her suffer . . . any more.' Her voice broke slightly.

He nodded his understanding.

The baby was asleep in her arms. She rose and walked over to the cot and laid him down, gently drawing the covers over him and touching his rounded cheek with a tender finger before returning to her seat by the fire.

Kyre produced his cigarette case and she accepted a cigarette with a faint smile and a nod of thanks. She bent her head over the flame of his lighter and exhaled a cloud of blue-grey smoke.

'Randall was at Oxford,' she said, composed again. 'He knew Simon — oh, not very well. They weren't exactly friends but they went to the same parties and belonged to the same clubs. I met Randall at a party last November. I went with a man I'd been going around with for some time — we were practically engaged and appearing together in a West End production. Randall was attentive but I didn't attach much importance to it . . . he had quite a reputation where women were concerned, you know — and I wasn't interested in being one more conquest. I didn't expect to meet him again after that night. But he began to haunt the theatre, telephone me, send me flowers and presents, pester me to go out with him. I kept refusing . . . he didn't attract me and Julian was still very much to the fore. Then Randall came to the flat I was sharing with another actress — he was waiting for me when I got back from rehearsal. I was rather blunt with him — and then he played his trump card. He knew all about my mother's death and unless I agreed to marry him he intended to take that knowledge to the appropriate authorities.' Her voice held bitter loathing and scorn.

'Your brother had told him?' He could not keep the astonishment from his tone.

She looked at the glowing end of her cigarette, turned it carefully between her fingers. 'Simon talks in his sleep at times — when he's excited or upset. They'd been to a party and Simon had too much to drink. Randall hauled him back to his rooms and put him to bed — and as it was late and he was a bit muzzy himself decided to sleep on the sofa. He heard Simon talking in his sleep . . . he'd had a letter from me that day and it was still very recent so I suppose he had my mother's death very much on his mind. Randall put two and two together — and challenged Simon the next day and got the whole story out of him . . . acting the part of the loyal friend who wouldn't let it go any further, I expect,' she added contemptuously. 'I suppose Simon was only too relieved to get it off his chest. He was always sensitive, easily upset, a bit broody over things. Randall made a note of everything . . . my name, my mother's name, the date of her death, the amount of tablets I'd given her, the name of the doctor . . . anything that might be useful at a later date. He carried a little book with such information and he showed me the relative page. I wasn't the only person in the book, of course. It was like a hobby to him — and he rather enjoyed being able to hold something over a person's head.'

Kyre could scarcely believe his ears. It did not sound like the boy he had known and loved — yet he could not discredit her story. 'But . . . it was a form of blackmail,' he said incredulously.

She gave her taut little laugh. 'It was blackmail. Randall's little speciality. He enjoyed it — and it brought him extra income.' There was a hint of scorn in her grey eyes as she turned to look at him. 'I told you that you didn't really know him . . . that he wasn't as perfect as you and the others seem to think.'

He wrinkled his brow thoughtfully. 'So you married him?'

'Yes. Oh, I know what you're thinking now. Why didn't he use his knowledge to get me to sleep with him? Why did he bother to marry me? I've often wondered about that, too — but as I told you I think he believed himself in love with me at the time . . . and he was very keen on the idea of having a son.' Her lip curled suddenly. 'Too bad he didn't live to enjoy the realisation of that ambition.'

Kyre said slowly: 'I believe you, of course, Sara. But it's a shock to be told that kind of thing about someone I'd known and loved since he was born.'

'I'm sorry,' she said abruptly. 'It isn't pleasant when illusions are destroyed. But you should know the truth. You were shocked to realise how little I cared that Randall was dead — how much I hated the thought of his child — how much I hated and despised the man I married. Now, I hope you understand my feelings a little.'

He leaned forward and stared into the fire, clasping his hands between his knees. 'It was monstrous of him to use his knowledge to force you into marriage with him . . . but if he loved you so much perhaps there is some excuse . . .'

'There isn't any excuse!' she interrupted swiftly, bitingly. 'He knew I detested him — it amused him to make love to me knowing that I shrank from the touch of his lips and hated the demands he made on me. You don't understand, Kyre,' she went on, more quietly and a little wearily. 'If he hadn't fancied himself in love and wanted to marry me, he would have used that knowledge in another way. Can't you understand? As soon as he realised that I was Simon Winston's sister and that he had the truth of my mother's death in his possession he knew that he had a weapon to use in any way he chose. He could have made me his mistress if he desired: he could have asked me for money; he could have made my life a misery in so many ways. And I wasn't the only one, Kyre! Try not to see him as a man who was your cousin and therefore entitled to your love and loyalty! He blackmailed people as a hobby — because he loved power and he loved money!'

His hands were clenched so tightly that the knuckles showed white. 'Have you proof that he blackmailed other people?'

'No . . . not absolute proof. But he always had money, Kyre — and I know people were afraid of him. A certain look in his eyes, a certain smile, a seemingly irrelevant remark — and then I knew that the person he was with had their name in his book and that they were either paying for his silence or that he was biding his time until it suited him! I'm not trying to blacken his character because I hated him — because he forced me to marry him! I want you to know what he really was. You don't believe me! I shouldn't have told you!'

He forced himself to smile. 'I'm glad you told me, Sara. It means that you trust me — and I want that more than anything.' He rose abruptly and placed a hand on her shoulder for a brief moment. 'I must think it over, Sara — it hasn't been pleasant hearing but I don't doubt your word.' He moved to the door and then paused as a thought crossed his mind. 'Do you know what happened to the book you mentioned — the book that Randall had with your name in it?'

She shook her head. She was suddenly very tired and vaguely unhappy.

'He always carried it with him.'

Kyre walked along the corridor to his own room, a deep furrow marking his brow and a grimness touching his eyes and lips.

No, he did not doubt Sara. There had been too much conviction in the quiet account, too much candour in her grey eyes, too much distress in her anxiety that he should believe what she told him . . .

11

Blackmail! It was an evil word and an evil occupation. Difficult to reconcile it with the charming, light-hearted, lovable Randall — and yet how much did one ever know of the secret personality of others, no matter how dear, how close they might be? Since he had grown up, Randall had spent more time away from the house than in it — and Kyre recalled now that his easy, careless chatter had always seemed to tell them everything yet told them very little. They had known almost nothing of his way of life in London or when he was at Oxford. They had known few of his friends. It was only too possible that Sara was speaking the truth. He had always been extravagant and careless with money. Kyre had paid out a staggering sum in bills since he left Oxford but it was possible that Randall had lived at a much faster pace than even those bills suggested.

He thought grimly that if Randall had been a blackmailer then his death must have been a relief not only to Sara but to other people who had reason to hate him . . .

He entered his room and walked across to a small writing-bureau. He unlocked it with a key that he carried on his chain and drew from a pigeonhole a small bundle. He had never given them more than a cursory glance since the day that the police had handed them to him when their enquiries were completed. At the time, he had put them in his bureau without checking through them but occasionally since then he had picked up the bundle and noted a few of its contents . . . driving licence, wallet, keys, a handful of letters that he had not read, an odd bill or two that Randall had evidently paid himself.

Now he was looking for a small, well-thumbed book — and he found it immediately. He sat down at the bureau and read it through systematically, a grave expression in his eyes. It confirmed everything that Sara had told him. He did not register the details of the peccadilloes that complete strangers to him had paid for time and again — but he noted with a tightening of the lips and a cold anger in his heart the dates and amount of the various payments. He took a sheet of notepaper and a pen and made a long list of names, addresses and figures.

The thing that shocked him most was that so many of the payments were for paltry sums . . . money that Randall could not have needed or really wanted — and this confirmed Sara's claim that he had enjoyed the sense of power even more than the handling of money. All the evidence seemed to point to the whole business being more of a hobby than anything else. The first recorded attempt at blackmail was during his Oxford days . . . the latest a date only two days before his death.

As he worked his way through the

small book, his anger grew colder and more lasting. He knew exactly what he intended to do ... burn this sorry record of a Hamilton's vicious streak and return the money anonymously to those who had paid for Randall's silence.

A name on the last page caught his eye — and he stiffened abruptly, a feeling of horror invading his entire being. The page contained no more than a list of names, dates and amounts ... nothing else to hint at the secrets that Randall had known. It was obvious that he had not needed to refresh his memory in these cases. As he read slowly down the page the last vestige of affection for his dead cousin dwindled slowly out of his heart and mind — and he tossed the book to one side of the bureau with a slow, contemptuous gesture.

He drew a cheque book towards him and the next hour was occupied in writing cheques and addressing envelopes. He thought grimly that it was certainly both fortunate and opportune that Purbrook had dealt so successfully with the American film studios for the sale of the film rights of his book.

When he had finished, he gathered up the pile of envelopes and slipped them into his pocket. Then he put the notebook in his pocket with the intention of throwing it into the boiler that provided the house with its central heating.

He walked back along the wide corridor and knocked lightly on the door of Sara's room. It was a moment or two before she replied and then she opened the door herself. She was dressed in a simple, dark wool dress and held a string of pearls in her hand. Her fine, flowing hair had been braided in a coronet and she had applied make-up with a skilful yet discreet hand.

He stared at her, unable to conceal his surprise — and suddenly seized with the fear that she meant to leave his house that very day.

She smiled at his expression. 'I

thought you wanted me to go down for dinner this evening,' she said lightly.

When he had left her, she had sat for some time before the fire, grateful for solitude. That first feeling of sadness and bitterness had gradually evaporated — and for the first time in almost a year she had been free of an intolerable burden. There had been no condemnation, no accusation in Kyre's manner as he listened to her story — and she was grateful and impressed by his compassion and understanding. He had not doubted her — and for that she was thankful, too. Whereas Randall had always succeeded in making her feel guilty and smeared with the horror of the murder she had committed, Kyre's quiet acceptance had restored her confidence and destroyed the sense of guilt. He understood: he sympathised: he knew her motives had been pure and unselfish and that only love and mercy had forced her to such an action.

She recalled his quiet, gentle request that she should join the family that evening — and she knew that by pleasing him she could repay him in some small measure for his kindness and his unstinted friendliness. So she had bathed and dressed and taken pains with her appearance for the first time in months. It had cost her some effort but she certainly felt all the better — and her heart was oddly light as she opened the door to him and recognised the flicker of appreciation and warmth in his dark eyes.

Relief swept through him. 'Why . . . yes, I should be very pleased,' he said unevenly. 'Are you sure that you're not tired — that you feel well enough?'

She certainly looked well, almost beautiful in that moment to him, the dark dress providing an excellent foil for her fairness and a surprising vivacity in her expression that he had never expected nor hoped to see. He knew abruptly why Randall had fallen in love with her, why he had chosen to marry her. There was a serenity, a purity, a glowing, untarnishable radiance that was seldom to be seen. Heart, mind and body instinctively responded to her quiet, moving appeal.

'I shall be all the better for leaving this room for a few hours,' she returned emphatically.

He looked about the room. 'Would you like to move into one of the others, Sara? I'll tell Mrs. Nunhead to prepare another room. This is not a woman's room.'

'It was Randall's, wasn't it?' she asked bluntly.

'Yes.'

'It doesn't really make any difference. One room is much like another. But I would like his books and brushes to be taken away. Do you mind?'

'Of course not. It was rather a ridiculous gesture to leave his things as they were before his death.'

She nodded. 'It rather irritated me,' she admitted. 'Mrs. Nunhead dusts everything so reverently.'

He smiled. 'She's a sentimentalist.'

She fastened her pearls about her

neck. 'Adam is asleep but I don't really like leaving him alone.'

'I'll ask Carol to sit with him,' he said quickly.

She smiled at his reflection in the mirror. 'I'm a little nervous, Kyre.'

'Nervous? Of dining with the family? Surely not!'

'We needn't pretend with each other,' she said unexpectedly. 'They don't like me and they don't trust me, for some reason. It's ridiculous but sometimes I feel they're afraid of me . . . '

'That's merely because you don't know each other very well yet,' he said lightly. But he knew that she spoke the truth . . . the family were afraid and now he knew why! He wondered that he should have been so lacking in perception — the air of uneasiness, the wariness, the resentment and dislike and the compulsive visits to Sara's room all told their own story. Each of them was worried that Randall might have passed on to his wife the secret that in some way he had managed to discover — and because they did not know Sara very well they feared that she might be preparing to step into Randall's shoes. Knowing Sara in a way that he had never known Randall, Kyre knew how fantastic and impossible that likelihood must be.

She turned to him, her mouth lifting slightly with that faintly mischievous smile that he was already beginning to recognise and love. 'I thought my tongue had something to do with it. I haven't been very pleasant to any of them during my stay.'

'You've had a rough time,' he said gently. 'No one will judge you by anything you said or did so soon after Adam was born.'

She placed a hand impulsively on his arm. 'How nice you are! You're not in the least like Randall!'

His heart lifted at the touch of her hand and at the impulsive, sincere warmth in her voice. 'I deem that a great compliment,' he said quietly. 'By the way, I came back to tell you what I mean to do.' He produced the notebook and the envelopes and explained his intentions briefly and concisely.

Sara listened and agreed, thinking that it was just what she should have known he would do. He was a man of integrity and honour, a man to be trusted, a man to admire and respect — and even to love, the thought flashed into her mind. She chased it away swiftly, chiding herself for even thinking of him in that light. He was virtually engaged to another woman, for one thing. For another, it was most unlikely that he thought of her as anything but his cousin's widow who had made an unfortunate marriage and meant to put the memory of it behind her as soon as possible. He would be kind and concerned and generous because these things were a part of his nature — but it would be very foolish to attach any importance to the warmth of his eyes, or voice, or smile when he was with her. In any case, surely she had experienced enough dealings with the Hamiltons without complicating matters by indulging in romantic fancies where Kyre was concerned!

She said abruptly: 'If you mean to pay back the money anonymously why are you sending signed cheques?'

He looked blank for a moment. Then he laughed. 'I hadn't thought of that, Sara. I don't think it would be a good idea to send cash so I shall have to enclose a brief note explaining that I've only recently come across a list of my cousin's debts and apologising for the delay in returning their generous loans. That should suffice. They may suspect that I know the truth — but at least I'm not asking them for money and that should relieve their minds. God knows they haven't much reason to trust anyone with the name of Hamilton but I hope they'll be able to read between the lines of my letter.'

'I'll help you write the letters, if you like,' she volunteered, a little shyly.

'Would you? I should be grateful,' he said quickly. His eyes held hers for a long moment then he looked away. 'I wish I could recompense you in some way, Sara.'

'Please . . . it wasn't a pleasant experience but it didn't last long — and Adam is all the recompense I want,' she said hastily . . .

To say that the Hamiltons were amazed by Sara's descent on Kyre's arm is to put it very mildly indeed. They simply stared, stunned to stillness like a tableau of statues. The slow colour began to rise in Sara's cheeks and she was grateful for the reassuring pressure of Kyre's hand and his swiftly-spoken, light: 'I've persuaded Sara to join us for dinner. It's very depressing for her to spend her evenings in her room alone.'

Cathryn was the first to remember her manners. She came forward with a swift, warm smile. 'How nice! You look very much better, Sara.'

Uncle James, a little red in the face, motioned Kane towards the decanters. 'I expect the young lady would like a drink Kane. Give her a glass of sherry

— it will bring some colour into her cheeks.' As she was already flushed with embarrassment his remark was neither appropriate nor tactful.

Honor studied Randall's widow with a keen, penetrating scrutiny. She noticed Kyre's solicitude, his smile, the look in his eyes — and decided that it was as well that she was leaving Hamilton House on the following day. Kane was right: Kyre would never marry her — for in all the years that she had known him he had never looked down at her with that particular tenderness in his eyes, never displayed so much protective concern for her well-being. She was angry with herself rather than with Kyre. She had thoroughly wasted her time and efforts and her only gain was the memory of Kane's kisses and caresses and endearments . . .

Aunt Dimity hurried forward, urging Kyre to install Sara in the most comfortable chair, close to the fire and away from any possible draught. She hovered anxiously with an armful of cushions, suggested that the tapestried footstool should be brought down from her own room for Sara's use, begged Sara not to tire herself — and yet for all her vague, sweet concern her faded yet keen eyes were anxious and shrewd as they darted from Sara to Kyre and back again.

Kane brought her the sherry. Philip, at a glance from his wife, hurried forward to offer the cigarette box. Uncle James fiddled with a box of matches. Cathryn drew her to talk of the baby and Melanie added her contribution to the conversation.

Honor watched with a faint curling of her lip, wondering at their concern and display of insincere affection and interest. Even Kane seemed to be dancing attendance and she had not expected that of him.

Kyre stood back, watching the group, a strange compassion and bewilderment in his eyes. What paltry, unimportant little secrets had they nursed to themselves throughout the years that were vital enough to any of them for Randall to benefit? Aunt Dimity with her gentle sweetness, her inconsequential chatter, her timidity and shyness — he could not imagine that she had anything to hide. Uncle James, bluff and blustering, a romantic liar with the wanderlust in his veins — undoubtedly there had been adventures and escapades but surely none so nefarious that a blackmailer could benefit? Mclanie . . . his glance strayed to his sister — her life was an open book to him — or so he had always believed yet Randall had learned something which she had paid for him to keep to himself! Kane — his twin despite the fact that they had never been intimates: women had always been his weakness; was it a long-forgotten, long-finished affair that might cause a scandal if it came to light? Cathryn . . . surely she was too young to have the kind of secret that Randall had sought to discover — what could he possibly have known about his sister that he had used to his own advantage — and why had he stooped so low as to extort money from the sister who loved and trusted him?

He did not wish to know their secrets. He merely wanted them all to know that they had nothing to fear from Sara — even if she knew their secrets which he doubted. She would surely have hinted — possibly, with candour, admitted that Randall had taken her into his confidence.

He was suddenly aware of Honor's gaze and he turned with a smile. 'I'm sorry . . . you haven't been introduced to Sara, of course!' He took her by the elbow and led her over to the fireplace, making his way through the members of his family who crowded about Sara's chair. He made the introduction and the two women exchanged pleasantries that were suitable to the occasion — while they assessed each other in truly feminine fashion.

Sara quickly formed an opinion that

was neither favourable nor complimentary. She had not expected that Kyre would consider marriage with a woman so cold, so hard, so sophisticated, so obviously born to rule and possess. But she reminded herself that Kyre's marriage was not her affair and felt compelled to be courteous if nothing else to Honor Pattison.

'Honor and I are very old friends,' Kyre said, smiling at the tall, sophisticated woman by his side — and there was a hint of long intimacy, of warm friendliness, of secret understanding in that smile that brought an almost physical sickness to Sara. Surely she could not be jealous of this unknown woman who had a claim to Kyre's affection and trust and understanding? Surely she was not flooded with bitterness merely because the cool, haughty, self-possessed Honor was to marry a man who could never turn marriage into mockery, love to hatred — and she had been compelled into a life with a man without morals or principles, kindness or real warmth?

She forced herself to smile, too, to say with just the right amount of interest: 'I've heard so much about you, Miss Pattison.'

If this woman was going to marry Kyre, then she had to be polite, friendly, at ease — for she must not antagonise Kyre in any way and she sensed that his loyalty was one of the finest and firmest facets of his character. She needed his friendship, his liking — even his affection if she were fortunate enough to win it. She needed to feel that she would always be a welcome visitor to Hamilton House if she chose to make her way there — at least where Kyre was concerned, she thought, as she recognised veiled hostility behind Honor's pleasantries. She reminded herself that she was a trained actress, that it should not be difficult or impossible to reach terms of seeming friendship with Kyre's future wife.

'Oh . . . but you haven't met Philip either,' Melanie said quickly — and Sara was glad of the interruption as she turned with a smile for the tall, slightly embarrassed Philip. She was not surprised by his stilted remarks, the faint reserve of his manner, the slight shiftiness of his expression — it was all of a piece with the behaviour of everyone else in this strange house!

It was a difficult, constrained meal. Uncle James was too hearty, too much the kindly uncle, oddly reticent on the subject of his adventures in other countries. Aunt Dimity was nervous, fumbling with cutlery, slightly deaf to oft-repeated requests for salt or bread, silent and obviously unhappy. Philip talked too much with a strange air of bravado and Melanie was on edge, frequently interrupting her husband, blatantly changing the subject whenever it chanced on America or Philip's work or the early days of their marriage. Honor was too sophisticated, too brightly talkative, too possessive in her manner — as though she sought to emphasise the difference between herself and the girl who toyed with her food, was extremely conscious of the strain and tension in the room and felt very much the outsider without Kyre's attentiveness to draw her into the family circle. And Kyre was preoccupied throughout the meal . . . watchful, noting the odd behaviour of his family, listening and wondering, thinking of what he must do very soon to set their minds at rest.

Kane was silent and sullen, directing many a bitter, mocking glance at Honor who ignored him completely, restless in the company of the girl who might well know of his long deception of his brother and fancying that she had only joined them that evening in order to expose him. Cathryn was annoyed with Kyre: obviously having invited Sara to join them she thought that he might make some effort to entertain her, to draw her into the conversation and put her at ease — or else spared them all the ordeal of a difficult hour. She was surprised to feel a certain sympathy for Sara . . .

Honor was vaguely at a loss. Before dinner, she had been almost convinced that Kyre was attracted to the stranger and that she might as well give up all hope of marrying him one day. Now, with his inattention to Sara, his seeming indifference to her shyness and discomfort, she wondered if his solicitude and warmth had been mere courtesy to a guest. Perhaps she had nothing to fear from the girl after all. Perhaps it would be unwise to throw in her hand just yet. Kyre was attractive, kind and considerate — and extremely wealthy. He might never stir her to the passion that she had experienced in Kane's arms. He might never be as exciting, as interesting, as stimulating and as demanding as Kane — and there might be difficult moments in the future if she persuaded Kyre into marriage and found herself living indefinitely beneath the same roof as his brother. But she had clung to the hope of marrying Kyre for too long to dismiss the idea completely — and why shouldn't he marry her? The property was entailed and he would need an heir one day. The thought of having a child was extremely distasteful to her but she would carry out a necessary evil with a show of interest and warmth. They had been friends for many years and she believed that Kyre had a certain amount of affection for her — as much as he was capable of knowing for any woman, anyway, she thought cuttingly, recalling his coolness and reserve of many occasions. Perhaps she had been too patient too long: perhaps Kyre was a man who needed to be more or less forced into a proposal of marriage; and surely she was experienced enough to handle the matter with competence?

12

After the meal, they adjourned to the sitting-room. It was not long before Melanie and Philip made their excuses and escaped to their own wing and the privacy and reassurance of their own company.

Aunt Dimity confessed to being tired and went off to her own room — and very shortly afterwards Uncle James declared that he had letters to write and followed his sister from the room.

Kyre smiled to himself without humour. 'And then there were five,' he murmured beneath his breath.

Kane went from the room to make a telephone call and returned a few moments later to state bluntly that he was going out to join some friends at the Country Club. He glanced at Honor with a small, unpleasant smile playing about his lips — and then turned on his heel. She stifled a sigh, wishing that she were going with him, wondering if he had thought for a moment of inviting her to do so — and yet knowing that he had not, that he had only mocked her enforced stay in the house.

Cathryn ruffled the pages of a magazine listlessly. Kyre fingered the small book in his pocket and remembered his intention to throw it into the furnace. Honor wandered to the decanters and poured herself another drink and Sara sat nervously on the edge of a chair and wondered if Carol was coping with Adam and if she could use her natural anxiety as an excuse to return to her room.

Kyre glanced at his cousin. 'Why not play something for us, Cathryn?' he suggested, nodding towards the piano.

She forced a smile. 'Oh, I don't think so. I'm not in the mood. I think I'll have an early night, if no one minds?'

'And then there were three,' Kyre said quietly and a little grimly.

'What was that?' Cathryn said, glancing at him.

'Nothing . . . I was merely quoting an old nursery rhyme,' he said with a faint, ironic smile.

She looked puzzled but merely picked up her magazine and went from the room with a cursory goodnight to the room in general.

Honor sipped her drink and looked at Kyre over the rim of her glass with a light of amusement in her eyes. 'Ten little niggers, I presume?' she asked lightly.

Sara half-rose. 'Would you mind if I went up, too, Kyre? I'm worried about Adam — and it is getting close to the time for his feed.'

'By all means,' he said, a little wearily. He glanced at his watch. 'I suppose I might as well adjourn to the study and do some work — if you mean to have an early night, too, Honor?'

She gave a light, brittle laugh. 'Oh, but I'm not tired, darling. And we don't have many opportunities to be alone, do we?' She neatly introduced a note of intimacy and the smile she directed to Sara deliberately conveyed thanks for her tact in leaving them and a hint of mutual understanding.

Sara coloured slightly. 'I'm sorry . . . I would have gone up some time ago . . . but . . . ' She trailed off as Kyre turned to her swiftly, almost impatiently.

'Don't be silly, Sara. No one wants you to sit on your own if you'd rather stay down here. There's another hour until Adam needs feeding, surely? Perhaps we could have some music — or a game of cards.' He was annoyed with Honor for the blatant indication that Sara's presence could be dispensed with.

Sara shook her head. She was not a fool — and it was only too obvious that she had been playing gooseberry unnecessarily. It was perfectly natural that Kyre and Honor should wish to be alone — and the others had been tactful enough to realise it. After all, Honor was returning to London the next day and it might be some time before she and Kyre had another chance to be together. 'No, I won't stay,' she said simply. 'I'm really rather tired . . . my nights are rather broken at the moment and I'm still supposed to rest as much as possible. Goodnight, Honor . . . goodnight, Kyre.'

The door closed quietly behind her and Honor moved lightly across the room to Kyre's side. 'I'm afraid she was a little embarrassed,' she said sweetly. 'She's little more than a child, darling — rather a surprising girl for Randall to have married. He always seemed to like the sophisticated type of woman.'

'Yes . . . well, I expect he wanted a change,' he said, almost curtly.

She pretended to ignore his annoyance. 'Odd that Randall should have been the first to marry,' she commented smoothly. 'I always thought of him as the bachelor type.'

He nodded. 'So did I.'

'Certainly I didn't imagine that he

would beat us to the altar,' she said with a little, confident laugh.

He glanced at her swiftly. This was a new approach — and rather blatant for a woman like Honor. She had never presumed to accept their marriage as a foregone conclusion — never taken for granted the proposal that he had never brought himself to make — never spoken as though they had already set the date for their marriage. He did not know how to deal with this approach. He was surprised that she still thought of him in connection with marriage, having convinced himself that she and Kane were lovers and that she had ceased to regard him as a possible husband. But it seemed that he would have to revise his views. If she cared at all for Kane, she could not wish to marry him ... yet would she have allowed Kane to make love to her if she did not care? Or had he leaped to false conclusions?

'No, nor did I,' he compromised — and realised immediately that he had played into her hands. His words could only be construed as an agreement with her surprise.

She smiled up at him warmly and slipped her hand into his arm. 'I don't know why we've waited so long, darling,' she said caressingly. 'It seems so silly to postpone our happiness like this. Randall has been dead for six months now . . . I don't think anyone would think our wedding in bad taste if it was arranged for next month.'

'Next month,' he repeated dully, his brain scurrying in an effort to disillusion the woman who had suddenly and unexpectedly shown a determination to marry him at all costs.

'Why not?' she asked lightly. 'It doesn't have to be a big affair.'

'Honor . . . do you want to marry me?' he asked abruptly.

'Of course I do, darling. I've never wanted anything else,' she said gently and reached to kiss his cheek, sliding her arms about him. 'I wondered when you would get around to asking me,' she teased indulgently — and his heart sank. 'Of course, we've always known that we'd be married one day — but I suppose we've been content to drift. Now . . . well, frankly, darling, I'm not getting any younger and I want to give you children . . . a son, at least.'

'I . . . I thought you didn't care for children,' he protested.

She raised startled eyes to him. 'Oh, but I do, Kyre! I love children . . . surely that's obvious! And I shall love your children even more.' She snuggled against him, resting her head on his shoulder, her eyes hard and angry now that he could not see their depths, furious that he was able to resist the melting warmth of her body and the invitation of her embrace.

Reluctantly Kyre put his arms about her and rested his cheek against that glossy raven hair. He had no love for Honor . . . affection, friendship, liking — but no love. He could not bear the thought of spending the rest of his life with her as his wife . . . not while his heart belonged to the girl who had so recently entered his life. This is all wrong, his heart raged within him. This should be Sara in my arms, Sara's head on my shoulder, Sara's pale hair beneath my lips, Sara's quiet, still voice murmuring endearments and speaking of a shared future. Yet how could he tell Honor with blunt cruelty that he did not love her, that he did not wish to marry her, that he did not welcome the thought of children that Sara did not bear . . . she was confessing her love and her longing, her dreams of the happiness they would know, making plans for the future — and he could not destroy those dreams and plans, could not scorn the offer of her love — a love he had always suspected but hoped would fade for want of encouragement during the last few years. Once, he would have welcomed these endearments, these loving arms, this candid discussion of marriage — when he had been seriously contemplating a life spent with Honor and thought that they could make a success of marriage. But time had taught him that they were not really suited to each other, that he could never love her and therefore could not enter into marriage with a sense of fitness, of justice, of integrity. Perhaps he had always considered the possibility that she would transfer her affections to Kane — a man so much better suited to her temperament, her character, her way of life, her thoughts and feelings.

He could not respond to the passionate nature of this woman. He could not force a warmth to his lips and sincerity to endearments that hovered, stillborn, on his tongue. So he stood, tense, ill at ease, seeking for an escape — while she held him close and talked eagerly, happily, of their wedding and their future.

At last she released him and stepped back. 'So it's really settled, dearest? Next month we'll be married — and live happily ever after!' Her eyes were glowing with triumph, the flush of satisfaction touched her cheeks — and only her heart was cold and contemptuous as she looked at him.

She would not admit, even to herself, that she had forced Kyre into the arrangements for their long overdue wedding merely to spite Kane, to punish him, to hurt him as he had hurt her. She told herself that Kane was a piece of easily-forgotten, easily-dismissed folly, that she had made up her mind to marry Kyre and would not be swerved from that intention, that she had succeeded in her aim to marry a man who was not only wealthy but famous in the world of literature, a man who could give her all she wanted from life.

Unsmiling, he nodded. 'If it's what you want, Honor.' Then, hastily, fearing that his indifference might hurt and banish the glow from her eyes. 'You're right ... we have waited too long darling. I should have realised how much I've missed all these years.'

She smiled, satisfied. She knew that he had no wish to marry her, that he did not love her — but he would not try to escape now. He was too honourable, too kind, too compassionate — and he would go through with it rather than inflict an imaginary hurt on the woman who seemed so eager to marry him.

She kissed the tips of her fingers to him. 'Now, to prove that I shall be an understanding wife, you are free to work if you must. I want to pack ready for the morning. But I shall be back very soon, of course — there is so much to arrange now. I wish I hadn't made so many appointments for the next few weeks . . . of course I could cancel them in the circumstances . . . '

'No,' he said swiftly. 'No, don't do that, darling. It may be some time before you meet all your friends again once you're married to me — I shall probably be a very possessive and somewhat selfish husband, wanting to spend all my time with you.'

When he was alone, he sank into a chair and buried his dark head in his hands. His faithful spaniel nuzzled his knee and whimpered her sympathy until he eventually dropped his hands and smiled reluctantly. He pulled her ears affectionately — but his thoughts were far from the dog at his feet.

He could not believe that he was really pledged to marry Honor. But it seemed to be an inescapable fact. She had manoeuvred him into a position where he had no choice but to fall in with her every suggestion. It was entirely his own fault. He should have made it clear long ago that he did not love her, that he would not marry her, freed her to seek a husband elsewhere instead of encouraging her to hope, to love, to use their close friendship as a lever to marriage.

He could not prevent his thoughts from straying to Sara. No doubt she was alone but for her baby, cradling him in her arms, crooning to him gently, pouring out all the love that had been stifled in her for so long. Kyre longed to go to her, to kneel at her feet, to know the tenderness of her arms about him and the comfort of her quiet voice, to confess his dilemma and seek her advice. But to do that would be to confess his love for her — and it was too soon, too presumptuous, too certain of failure. She would be startled, confused — and she would leave this house never to return. That must not happen. He would make no move to stop her from leaving if she wished . . . but he would do all in his power to ensure that she came back from time to time. It would be little comfort to have her beneath his roof, loving her, wanting her, irrevocably tied to another woman — but his life would be empty, hopeless, if he could not be with her occasionally . . .

He determined to think of other things . . . and thrust his hand into his pocket for his pipe. Contacting the small, black book he drew it out, looked down at it for a long moment and then abruptly consigned it to the flames of the fire. It burned fitfully at first and finally caught — and he watched and stirred it with a poker until nothing but ashes remained.

Then he rose with a certain resolution in his movement, crossed to his desk and wrote out five cheques with a determined expression. Then he pocketed the cheques and went from the room . . .

He knocked lightly and at first Aunt Dimity did not hear him. But she heard the second knock and bade him enter. He smiled reassuringly as she turned a wary face.

'I don't intend to stay more than a few minutes, Aunt Dimity,' he said lightly. 'I know it's late.'

'My dear boy, I'm pleased to have your company. Do sit down.' And she hurried to remove her knitting from a chair and plumped the cushions and waved him towards it.

He hesitated — and then decided that he could not simply thrust a cheque into her hand and hurry away. So he sat down and smiled at her again.

'I've just found out that you were in the habit of lending Randall money, Aunt Dimity,' he said gently, easily.

'That was very naughty of you, you know. He had a generous allowance — and if he needed more he should have come to me. He had no right to worry you . . . to deprive you of the little that is your own.'

She blanched and began to tremble. 'Oh, but . . . it was so little, Kyre. And I was glad to give it to him. He was a foolish boy, always getting into debt — I was glad that I could help him. And he didn't like to ask you for more when you've always been so generous.'

Kyre sorted through the handful of cheques and passed one across to her. 'Well, it's ancient history now, Aunt Dimity. I believe that is the amount you gave Randall?'

She looked at the cheque, her frail hands shaking uncontrollably. She was still ashen, her blue eyes filling with tears. 'It was such a long time ago . . . You must despise me, Kyre — but I was so young, so inexperienced. I've lived with the shame of it for so many years . . .'

'It's over now, darling,' he said gently, patting her hand. 'Try to forget it.'

She shook her head. 'How can I? I hoped no one need ever know . . . Mother and I went to such pains. But Randall found out . . . I was young and silly — and young girls always kept a diary in those days. It was expected — but I didn't know it had slipped behind the books in the study. I thought it had been destroyed years ago and then Randall found it and learned that he was my grandson. Oh, he was so sweet, so loving — he was so pleased to know the truth and he always called me Grandmother when we were alone . . . such a dear boy but weak . . . like Kay. I didn't want Martin to marry her but I couldn't do anything about it . . . I was only his 'sister', you see.' The tears spilled and traced their way slowly down her crumpled cheeks.

Kyre stared at her — too stunned to do anything but listen, powerless to stem the flood of revelation.

'I couldn't refuse him the money,

could I? He was my grandson and I loved him — and he was so sweet, promised it was only a loan, that I would have it all back . . . '

'I don't understand, Aunt Dimity,' Kyre managed to say at last.

She looked at him uncertainly. 'But she told you . . . '

'Sara? No, she told me nothing. I'm sure she knows nothing. I doubt if Randall ever confided in her,' he said grimly.

'Then . . . how did you find out?'

'Randall kept a notebook with a record of the money he 'borrowed' — I found your name and decided to repay you myself,' he explained quietly.

'He had it written down? Then . . . anyone could have learned the truth?' she asked, horrified. Fresh tears began to flow. 'And I've been so terrified all these years that the family would find out . . . that my shame would be general knowledge.'

'Aunt Dimity, I don't know anything but what you've told me now. I don't understand — but it's still your secret and I've no intention of repeating any of this conversation to anyone,' he said firmly, reassuringly.

She held out her hand to him in silent appeal. He took it and pressed it gently, then raised it to his lips with a loving smile.

'You're a good boy,' she said slowly. 'Good blood — the Hamilton and the Grierson. Your mother was a fine woman . . . a lovely, kind and warm-hearted woman. I loved her dearly. Martin should have married a woman like your mother, Kyre. My poor Martin . . . my lovely boy . . . he was a beautiful baby and I adored him. That girl's little boy reminds me of my Martin, you know,' she sighed. 'It's hard, Kyre . . . hard to deny the truth, to still my foolish old tongue when I look down at my great-grandson.'

Kyre said wonderingly: 'Martin was your son, Aunt Dimity?'

She nodded. 'I was only twenty — a silly little miss without a thought in my head but flirtation. I was so innocent . . . criminally so! My poor mother was heartbroken — but she was wonderful to me. We went away to Switzerland . . . for my health, people were told — and when we came back my father was presented with another son. Only my mother and I knew the truth . . . even Father believed that Martin was his child.'

'But . . . the man . . . Uncle Martin's father?'

'Oh, he was married, of course. Much older — and very experienced — rather a dangerous man. Perhaps that's why I loved him so much. Because I did love him, Kyre dear — and I never loved anyone else. Of course, marriage was out of the question — a bride simply had to be innocent in those days. But I didn't want to get married . . . I had my Martin and I adored him and he was very much mine even though I had to accept him as a brother. No, I didn't want to marry anyone, Kyre.'

'And this was the secret that Randall discovered?'

'Yes. You see, I kept a diary — and Randall found it in the study. Old and faded but I always had a very clear, decisive handwriting . . .'

'But why did you . . . lend him money on the strength of it?'

Her faded blue eyes held bewilderment. 'Oh, my dear — you don't understand. It was a terrible sin — a terrible shame . . . not even the family could be told!'

Kyre rose, his mouth set in a grim line. 'Well, you've certainly paid all these years for something that my generation doesn't consider such a sin or shame, Aunt Dimity.'

'It was only the last few years . . . and it wasn't so much,' she protested. 'I didn't have very much . . .'

'I'm not talking about money — or Randall,' he broke in quickly. 'I mean that you couldn't enjoy your child or admit him openly as your son — and you've been denied the natural pleasure of being accepted as a grandmother by Randall and Cathryn.'

'Yes . . . that was very hard,' she said sadly.

'You know that I shall keep your secret, Aunt Dimity, don't you?'

She smiled tremulously. 'It doesn't seem to matter any more, Kyre . . . and I'd rather like that baby to know that I'm his great-grandmother. And Cathryn . . . my dear Cathryn — do you think she would condemn me?'

'Of course not!' He stooped to kiss the faded cheek. 'She couldn't love you any more than she does now, of course — but she would be thrilled and very happy to know the truth. You are her closest relative, after all.'

He left her, happier than she had been for a long time, and walked along the corridor, musing of the high moral standards of her generation and knowing a deep compassion for all that she had missed in life . . .

13

Uncle James threw open the door at his knock and welcomed him with affectionate enthusiasm. 'Glad to see you, my boy! Nice of you to spare me a few minutes — I know you're always busy. Come in . . . come in! Sit down! I'll get you a drink . . . I still have a few bottles of the wine I bought in Spain.'

Kyre refused the drink and produced the cheque. There was no need to beat about the bush with James Hamilton. 'I think that's the right amount, Uncle James. I wish you'd consulted me before giving Randall money, though . . . you haven't so much that you could afford to pay for his extravagances.'

The old man stared at the cheque, high, difficult colour mounting to his cheeks. 'So the girl *did* know,' he muttered. 'Thought she must . . . hm!

What's she been telling you, young man?'

'Nothing at all.'

'Nonsense . . . nonsense! How did you know about this money, eh? Must have told you everything!'

'She merely gave me an insight into Randall's hobbies that I found very enlightening. A record that he kept told me the rest.'

Fear leaped into his eyes. 'A record? You mean he wrote it down in a book? The damned young puppy. Why, anyone could have got hold of it!'

'Apparently they didn't . . . except for myself, of course — and there was nothing in the book . . . '

Uncle James interrupted him roughly, obviously shaken and ill at ease: 'So *you* know? Well, I hoped to keep it dark for the rest of my life. Not a nice story, eh? But over and done with — and I paid the penalty.' He reached for his stick and limped painfully across the room to the fire. 'I was always one for the women — like young Kane. Tell him to watch his step . . . they're not to be trusted . . . not the women he likes. I should know! Women — bah! I tangled with 'em once too often — and let the wench talk me into marrying her.' He chuckled reminiscently. 'Well, she was a fiery piece — dark and buxom and hot-blooded and I was mad to have her! So I married her — all right and tight. Or so I thought! How was I to know she had a husband and three children? Tell me that? How was I to know? Had the shock of my life when her husband turned up with a rifle.' He shot Kyre a sly, mischievous glance. 'So now you know the truth about this game leg of mine, don't you? No crocodile, no axe-swinging villain, no half-crazed horse! An irate husband with right on his side and a trigger-happy finger — and me with half a dozen bullets in my leg and a charge of bigamy staring me in the face. Might have killed me, the fool! Well, he didn't — and I left the country as soon as I could. It shook me — a man of my age falling for a pretty wench and being led to the altar like a calf to the slaughter. Knew it was a mistake before the week was out — the first time I'd admitted to being an old man . . . but I'm damned if I knew that I'd be hobbling on to a ship bound for England before the end of the month. That was a narrow escape . . . and no doubt they're still waiting to clap me in gaol if I ever go back to Jo'burg!' He bowed his head, peeping irrepressibly at Kyre from beneath his lashes. 'Not a nice story . . . didn't want it known — have the whole county laughing their heads off! Not to mention the police asking questions at the door! So I kept it dark — and persuaded Randall to keep his mouth shut, too . . . the young devil!'

Kyre listened, fascinated and rather amused. 'But how did he find out, Uncle James?'

The old man shook a fist. 'Prying little imp! I found him in here one day, looking through my private papers. He found some newspaper cuttings about the business — I shouldn't have kept them, of course — but she was an attractive wench and the photographs did her justice. I liked to take them out and look at her photographs — and remember those few weeks we had together,' he admitted, a little sheepishly. 'No fool like an old fool, my boy!'

Kyre felt a surge of affection for the old man. 'She led you up the garden path, Uncle James.'

He chuckled. 'Yes, she did — the little . . . well, ancient history can't interest you, Kyre. I had my fun and I don't regret it . . . but I didn't want the story bandied about.' There was a note of anxiety in his voice.

'Don't worry, Uncle James. It won't be — I can keep a still tongue in my head. But I do wish that you'd come to me when Randall asked you for money . . . I'd have settled the matter immediately.'

'Yes . . . and Randall would have enjoyed recounting the story far and wide,' the old man said shrewdly. He smoothed out the cheque in his hand. 'I couldn't really afford this . . . but I had no choice, as I saw it. You do understand?'

'Yes, of course. Put that cheque somewhere safe — and pay it into your account tomorrow. As far as I'm concerned the whole affair is closed — and I shall never mention it again.'

He nodded a courteous goodnight and went from the room, smiling to himself as he walked along the corridor. He could not imagine the intrepid James Hamilton, the fearless handler of savage crocodiles, the no-nonsense settler of an axe-swinger's hash, the courageous tackler of wild horses, caught in a compromising situation with another man's wife and forced to run for his life with a zinging rifle on his heels, hiding in corners and watching for the zealous police while he waited for a passage on a boat that would remove him from the scene of his crime . . . if crime one could believe it to be! Poor old Uncle James . . . nursing the memory of perhaps the only love of his life that had ended so ludicrously and painfully!

The smile faded as he thought of Randall and the cold, cruel manner of his preying on the defenceless old pair. He had surely known that Aunt Dimity's sin had been expatiated long since and that no one could think badly of her part in an ancient scandal. He must have known that Uncle James' story would be thought as wild and as fantastic, as incredible, as all the others, causing only polite interest and secret amusement. Yet he had taken money from them and allowed them to live in constant fear of exposure!

He felt he could not stomach any more of Randall's petty vices that evening. He would tackle Melanie and Cathy and Kane the following day . . .

Kane came home very late that light. His noisy arrival disturbed Kyre and he pushed away his typewriter and went into the hall.

'You've obviously enjoyed your evening,' he said, trying to keep too blatant a reproof from his tone.

Kane grinned at him. 'Sure! More than you have, I'll wager! You and that ruddy typewriter! Don't you ever get tired of work — or is it too lucrative?' He had been drinking heavily in an effort to kill all thought of Honor — not very successfully.

'I'd suggest a drink — but I think you've had enough,' Kyre said smoothly.

'Yes, I've had more than enough . . . of you and this house and that bitch of a woman! You're welcome to her . . . do you know that? She means to get you by fair means or foul — and you're fool enough to walk straight into her little web. You won't even have the guts to struggle — she knows that!'

Kyre said quietly: 'Don't be offensive.'

'You're welcome to that cold, arrogant bitch,' he repeated, swaying slightly on his feet. 'And you're just the man to make her realise her mistake!'

Kyre frowned. 'Mistake?'

'Because she prefers you to me — or think she does! It's your money she loves . . . not you! When it comes to loving — she likes my brand of kisses. God, but she's a beauty . . . if she dares to marry you I swear I'll kill her.'

He held out his hands and stared at them as though they were already red with her blood. They shook with the passion of his anger.

Kyre turned on his heel. 'Go to bed, Kane. You're drunk!'

He laughed vibrantly. 'Drunk with the memory of her lovely, white body . . . drunk on her kisses, her caresses. Drunk . . . I'd like to drink for ever at that fountain!'

Honor, disturbed by the noise and the unmistakable sound of Kane's voice raised in passionate anger, came out of her room, fastening her negligée. She paused at the top of the stairs, the colour rushing to her face as Kane's words came to storm her ears. He looked up and saw her, stumbled to the foot of the stairs and swept her a low, mocking bow.

'There's my beauty, my love, my passionate goddess!' he cried. 'Come to my arms, my sweet.'

She ran down the stairs, her face aflame, her dark hair falling about her shoulders and her eyes blazing with hot anger. 'Be quiet, you fool! How dare you say such things about me!'

Kyre looked at her steadily. 'How do you know he was talking of you, Honor? He's too drunk to make sense.' He did not doubt that she had heard most of his brother's inflamed remarks. He was not surprised that she associated herself with everyone of them.

She flashed him an impatient glance. 'I won't have him rousing the house with his nonsense, Kyre. Can't you get him up to bed?'

Kane held out his hands to her, his eyes sombre now with a quiet appeal. 'Honor, I'm not so drunk. Honor, couldn't you try to love me?'

'For heaven's sake . . . '

'I love you . . . I swear I do! You don't want to marry a cold fish like Kyre . . . he'll never make you happy. You need a man like me . . . Honor, you can't go to him after giving yourself to me!'

She turned on him in a frenzy of rage, seeing all her careful plans shattering in the face of his unwise, thoughtless words. 'Shut up, you lying devil! That foul tongue of yours will make mischief one of these days! Kyre, you know he's drunk . . . he doesn't know what he's saying — it's absolute nonsense!'

Kane abruptly sat down on the bottom stair and buried his head in his hands. Honor looked at him with some impatience — and then his attitude of dejection, the oddly-moving curve of his cheek, the cluster of dark curls on the nape of his neck touched something within her to warmth.

With an oddly maternal tenderness, she sat down by his side and put her arms about him. 'Darling, go to bed,' she said gently. 'We'll talk in the morning.'

He turned to her and she let him draw her into his arms and bury his face in her shoulder. She stroked his dark hair and looked up at Kyre with a smile that was defenceless and yet defiant.

'I'm sorry,' she said quietly. 'You can see the way it is, Kyre.'

'You love him?' he asked, wondering at his astonishment. Of course she loved him — there was no other answer to her sudden change of heart, that tender warmth of eyes and mouth, the urge to comfort that was stronger than self.

'I suppose I do,' she said and her voice held a faint wonder. 'He needs me, anyway — and that matters to me, Kyre.' She turned to the man in her arms. 'Come, darling . . . '

He clung to her fiercely. 'You'll marry me?' He was harsh with the urgency of his need. 'I didn't mean the things I said to you . . . I was angry, bitter — and I love you so much.'

'Yes, I know.' She kissed him. 'We'll

talk about it in the morning.'

'You're going to London in the morning.' His voice held the petulant note of a child suspicious of a promised treat.

She smiled. 'No, I won't leave you, Kane. We'll be married as soon as possible.'

He put her aside, abruptly sober, and rose to his feet. He met Kyre's eyes with an intrepid honesty. 'It doesn't matter to you? You don't want her, do you?'

Kyre was at a loss. Honor supplied his answer with a faint smile: 'No, he doesn't want me, darling. He never did. I knew that years ago. Kyre and I are friends — nothing more.'

Kane went on, his face darkening slightly with embarrassment: 'I've been cheating you for years, Kyre. Five thousand pounds in my bank account belongs to you . . . I've been falsifying the accounts, laying up money so I'd have sufficient to persuade Honor that her happiness was with me instead of you. She's used to money, you see

286

— she wouldn't want to marry a man without it . . . '

'I do now,' she said firmly. 'My thousand a year and your allowance will keep us comfortably.'

Kyre stared at his brother. 'Five thousand pounds . . . but how could you . . . you couldn't possibly transfer five thousand from my account into your own without my knowledge!'

Kane nodded. 'It was easy. You weren't very interested in the accounts and never bothered to check them. I could show you a handful of bills and ask you for a cheque — and you never wanted to see the bills, some of which had been paid months before. You trusted me, I know — and I let you down time and again. I've been doing it ever since I took over the estate management. I've always wanted Honor, you see . . . I'll write you out a cheque in the morning.'

Kyre smiled at his twin — that warm, rather sweet smile of his that could melt the coldest heart and still the fiercest anger. 'Call it square . . . a wedding present, if you like.'

Kane shook his head. 'I can't do that . . .'

Kyre silenced him with a firm grip of his hand on his brother's shoulder. 'We'll talk about it in the morning,' he said quietly — and went into the study and closed the door with a little snap of finality.

His first feeling was one of relief . . . he need not marry Honor, after all. He did not understand why she had suddenly chosen to manoeuvre him into agreement — but no doubt Kane had something to do with her action. Now, he was still free to love where he pleased — and his heart had impulsively settled that for him. His love might never know the fulfilment of its hopes — but time was a great healer and one day Sara might forget her bitterness and turn her thoughts to the man who truly loved her. There were ways and means of proving his love — and he would not hesitate to follow them, always remembering her shy, sensitive nature. He knew that she had a heart that ached to love and be loved — she was like a ship without an anchor, without a harbour, but in time she might recognise his willingness to provide both anchor and harbour and surround her with the warm, comforting, reassuring sea of his love . . .

The money that Kane had admitted to appropriating thoughout the years was unimportant although it was a shock to discover that he was capable of long deceit. But he was already growing immune to such shocks . . . he had thought that he knew the characters and vagaries of each member of his family but circumstances had proved otherwise. He thought a little sadly of Shakespeare's words: *Conscience doth make cowards of us all . . .*

It was obvious now why Kane had been giving money to Randall: obviously the boy had found out in some way that Kane was defrauding the estate and demanded payment for his silence.

So that was another strand of the mystery unravelled.

Yawning mightily, he allowed himself the luxury of a last pipe before seeking his bed . . . and the luxury of contemplating a future in which he might find his long-awaited happiness with the woman he loved . . .

There was an immediate change in the atmosphere on the following day. Uncle James was in high good humour and enlivened the breakfast table with a recital of his adventures in China. Catching Kyre's eye, he coloured a little and gave a sheepish smile — and then as Kane urged him on continued with his story. Aunt Dimity entered the room, humming softly, her eyes bright, and immediately drew Melanie into a discussion of the little matinee coat she was knitting for the new baby in the house.

Honor and Philip were talking amicably together and for the first time she encouraged him to discuss his artistic efforts and promised to get in touch with a friend who kept an Art Gallery in Bond Street and might be persuaded to take an interest in Philip's work. It was obvious to Kyre that she already thought of herself as a Hamilton and intended to do her best for every member of that family — and it pleased him to note her happiness, the serenity in her eyes. It seemed that having finally surrendered to the undeniable truth of her love for Kane she did not seek to hide it from the world — their exchange of glances, their smiles, the hint of intimacy in their voices when they spoke to each other blazoned the rightness of their engagement. It had not yet been announced to the family — but their usual good terms were so heightened that Kyre felt that an announcement would prove to be unnecessary.

Cathryn came in late, her eyes dancing, a flush of happiness in her cheeks and a letter clutched tightly in her hand. She murmured a greeting absently and slipped into her seat, refusing everything but coffee — and hugging a secret knowledge to herself.

Kyre was impatient to have the meal over. Sara still took breakfast in her room and he wished to see her to talk to her, enjoy an hour of her company before he went to the typewriter.

As it happened, he rose from the table as Cathryn pushed back her chair — and he decided to take the opportunity of a few minutes alone with her. So he slipped an arm about her shoulders as they went towards the door and said lightly: 'Are you rushing off — or can you give me a few minutes of your time?'

She hesitated. 'I have a letter to write . . . but it can wait for the moment, I suppose. What is it, Kyre? Something important?'

He threw open the door of the study. 'You seem very happy this morning.'

She preceded him into the room. 'Oh, I am,' she said, smiling and fingering the letter that lay in the pocket of her slacks.

'Good news?' he asked, his eyes touched with warm affection as he looked down at her.

'The very best!'

He went to his desk and picked up the cheque he had made out in her name. 'Then this will help you to celebrate.'

She looked at it in surprise. 'Why . . . what's this, Kyre? Why are you giving me this money?'

'Because I'm responsible for Randall's debts — and that's the amount he owed you, I believe.'

The colour fled swiftly from her cheeks . . . and then, as she remembered the letter which made everything wonderful again, ebbed back again and she laughed with sheer happiness. 'Oh, that!'

'Yes . . . that, darling,' he said quietly.

Her eyes twinkled with mischief. 'So Sara knew all the time . . . I thought she might. But it doesn't matter now, Kyre — she can't hurt him with her knowledge now!'

He gestured with slight impatience. 'Everyone seems to have viewed Sara as a threat to their peace of mind. I assure you that she knew nothing about this money, Cathryn.'

'Then how did you find out?' she challenged.

He shrugged. 'Randall was a very methodical man.'

She looked at him quickly. 'Meaning that he kept records?'

'In a sense.'

'I see . . . Well, I've had a letter from Charles this morning. His wife died last month and he still loves me! So we can be married — without any scandal or any threat to his career. Oh, not immediately, of course — no breath of suspicion must attach to our marriage. But we will be married!'

Kyre frowned, bewildered by her impulsive, happy flow of words. 'I'm completely in the dark, darling. Who is Charles?'

'Charles Latimer, of course.'

The name was familiar but he could not place it. 'Do I know him?'

'You know of him, darling,' she said, a

trifle impatiently. 'Charles Latimer, the specialist — he is rather famous, you know.'

He nodded, remembering. 'Yes, of course. And you say that you're going to marry him?'

'Now that he's free, of course. We've been in love for over a year. Divorce was out of the question — and we didn't even dare to meet. His wife was terribly jealous and possessive — and the slightest hint that he was in love with me would have meant the end of his career. Doctors aren't supposed to fall in love with their patients, you know.'

It came back to him with sudden clarity. Cathryn had fallen from her mount during a local hunt and injured her back eighteen months before. There had been a possibility that she might never walk again . . . but a friend had recommended Latimer and the famous specialist had operated skilfully and successfully. Cathryn had continued to see him for some time once she was well — but Kyre had never guessed that his cousin had concealed a secret love for over a year.

'Randall knew about this?'

She nodded, biting her lip. 'He found the one and only letter that Charles ever wrote to me . . . soon after we agreed not to see each other again until he was free. His wife was an invalid for years — she might have outlived him or she might have died at any time. We could only love each other and hope to be together one day. Randall knew that his letter could damage Charles in his career — and that his wife would seize on the letter as a confirmation of her suspicions. Not that she really had cause to suspect Charles . . . he had been a good and faithful husband for years but she had been ill for such a long time that it had affected her judgment. I gave Randall that money — and he returned my letter. But I couldn't be sure that he didn't make a copy — or that Sara didn't have it in her possession now.'

He nodded grimly. 'I see. So that explains your fear and dislike of poor

Sara — who has suffered enough this past year without meeting with such a poor welcome in this house.'

She was taken aback by the anger in his voice. 'Well, you can't blame me, Kyre. I had to protect Charles . . . and I had to find out if Sara knew anything about our affair. I haven't been unpleasant to her — I don't even dislike her, really. She has had a rough time, I agree, and I'm sorry for her.' Suddenly her eyes were mischievous again. 'I don't think she needs my sympathy, though . . . rough deal she may have had but it seems to have brought her the ace, after all.'

He could not mistake the meaning behind her words or the impish knowledge in her eyes. 'I hope she will think so,' he said quietly, making no attempt to deny her evident belief that he had fallen in love with the shy, unhappy, Sara.

14

They went from the room together — and met Melanie on her way across the hall, a determined set to her chin. 'Oh, Kyre . . . are you going out? I want to talk to you.'

Kyre paused. 'No, I was going to visit Sara. But it can wait.'

'Good. It won't take long.' She passed him and went into the study.

Kyre smiled down at Cathryn. 'I'm glad for you, darling,' he said gently. 'If it's really what you want . . . '

'Yes . . . more than anything in the world,' she said emphatically and he was content.

Melanie was waiting for him, her eyes resolute and a slight nervousness betrayed by the restlessness of her hands. 'Kyre, I need your advice,' she said. 'Randall was blackmailing Philip and I for years. I want to find out if Sara knows about it — and if Randall told her why. You're on good terms with her . . . you could find out discreetly.'

'I don't think Sara ever knew the secrets that Randall held in his keeping,' he told her bluntly. 'I'm glad you came to tell me, Melanie — you're the only one who has done so.' He held out the remaining cheque. 'This is the right amount, I believe. You shouldn't have given him so much, Melanie — this money is needed for other things. If you had come to me in the first place I could have ensured Randall's silence without money.'

She stared at the cheque. 'Then you knew all the time?'

'No. I wish I had known. I only found out about this yesterday.'

She sank into a chair. 'I suppose you think Philip should give himself up.' Her voice took on a note of defiance. 'Well, I don't intend to let him do it, Kyre. He's changed his name and there isn't any evidence that would stand up without his confession. I love him and we've been very happy — and we have the children to consider.'

He touched her shoulder with a gentle hand. 'I don't know what Philip has to hide — and I don't wish to know. I merely discovered that you'd given Randall money — and I'm giving it back to you now. Keep your secrets, Melanie.'

She fingered the cheque with nervous, jerky gestures. 'He was only a boy, Kyre . . . a silly, impulsive boy. He was frightened — he's still frightened and he needs me. I can protect him, look after him, make him forget . . . '

'No one need ever know,' Kyre said quietly. 'Randall knew . . . but he's dead. Don't worry about it any more, dear.'

She smiled tautly. 'I shall always worry. One day someone might see him . . . someone who knew him in America . . . someone who knows that he was mixed up in that bank robbery and that he fired the gun. A man was killed, Kyre . . . oh, he didn't mean to shoot him . . . he was frightened, a boy with a gun he didn't understand, mixed up in something he didn't like or understand. He was lucky . . . the police never suspected him. They never charged anyone with the murder of that bank guard . . . just another unsolved crime. Philip borrowed enough money to take him to South America and changed his name — but he didn't even feel safe there so he came to this country. He told me before we were married — but it didn't make any difference. I loved him, you see,' she finished simply.

Kyre listened to her recital in silence. He could not think of Philip as a murderer — or of his sister as an accomplice. He could only feel compassion — and a strong reluctance to know the truth. 'I didn't want to know,' he said quietly.

'But I wanted you to know,' she said. 'You're my brother — and I've carried the burden of Philip's secret too long. What will you do now?'

'Do? Nothing. I'm not Philip's

conscience,' he told her swiftly.

'And you're sure that Sara doesn't know?' Suspicion still touched her voice and attitude.

'Of course she doesn't! Surely you don't think she came here with the sole purpose of carrying on where Randall left off?'

'It's possible, isn't it?'

'No! Sara is incapable of that kind of thing — it revolts her. She suffered herself at Randall's hands, Melanie!'

She was startled. 'You mean . . . is *that* why she married him? He black-mailed her into marriage?'

'Yes. But don't ask me to reveal her secret because I've no intention of doing so,' he said firmly.

'I don't want to know,' she retorted arrogantly. 'But it does explain a lot of things.' She rose to her feet. 'Well, I must go back to Philip — and set his mind at rest.' She paused by the door and turned to look at him. 'I think we've spent enough of our married life in this house, Kyre. We mean to look for a house of our own . . . do you mind?'

He shook his head. 'No, Melanie — I think you are very wise. Philip will never make his way as an artist if things are always made easy for him. Perhaps he'll paint something that people will buy when it's a matter of providing for you and your children.' He spoke kindly but Melanie, with the instinct of her love, recognised that he knew and deplored her husband's weak character.

'You've done so much for him,' she said slowly. 'So much for us all, Kyre . . . '

The door closed behind her, leaving him to wonder if he had done too much for his family throughout the years. Perhaps he should have encouraged them all to stand on their own feet, to carve their own destinies, to make their own way in the world. He was abruptly conscious that soon he would be alone in the big house but for Uncle James and Aunt Dimity. Honor would not want to live here with Kane, knowing that she was not the mistress of

Hamilton House — and in his heart he knew that Kane would relinquish the handling of the estate, convinced that his brother would never wholly trust him again, knowing that he dare not trust himself when it had proved so easy to defraud the estate. Melanie and Philip would leave, with the two children, as soon as they had found a suitable house. Cathryn would marry her Charles and find her happiness in different surroundings despite her claim that the man she married would be content to live in the house which had always been her home. It was unlikely that Latimer would give up his lucrative career and there would be much to occupy Cathryn in town in the future.

Sara . . . would she really go back to London and the theatre, taking the boy with her? Or could he persuade her to stay?

At last he was free to mount the staircase and knock lightly on the door of her room. She came to open it and greeted him with a shy, uncertain smile.

'How are you this morning, Sara? Not too tired after last night?' Nervousness made him formal, slightly aloof.

Sensitive, she immediately took refuge in cool, almost hostile indifference. 'I'm well enough.'

'And the boy?'

She scarcely glanced at the cot. 'Oh, he's fine.'

'I've asked Mrs. Nunhead to bring coffee,' he said.

'Oh?' She walked to the window and stared without interest at the rolling acres of land.

Kyre wondered why she had withdrawn into herself, why the intimacy of the previous day seemed abruptly lacking. He went to stand by her side. It was a bright, clear day with that winter sunshine which is so deceptive in its promise of warmth.

'Nice to see the sun,' he said idly. 'It's a splendid view, isn't it?'

Sara glanced at him and recognised the loving pride in his expression. 'You love this land, don't you?'

He nodded, smiling. 'Yes, I do. It's belonged to Hamiltons for generations, you know. It's my heritage — and the heritage of my son.'

She knew that he spoke of a son yet to be born — and his words were a reminder of his eventual marriage. She could not like Honor Pattison and she was bewildered by a strange, almost frightening emotion which swept through her at the thought that the cold, hard woman would know the love and loyalty, the warmth and kindness, the tenderness and consideration of this man for the rest of her life. Suddenly weary and sick at heart, she leaned her brow against the cold pane of the window.

Kyre laid a hand on her shoulder in swift concern. 'Are you sure you feel well, Sara? You're very pale.'

She turned from the window. 'I'm always pale.' Her tone was flat, listless, oddly touching.

Kyre suppressed the desire to take her in his arms, to hold her close and murmur words of comfort . . . comfort for what he did not know. He only sensed that she was unhappy, perhaps lonely.

Mrs. Nunhead knocked and entered the room with the tray which she placed on a low table with a speaking glance for the man and woman. She acknowledged Kyre's nod of thanks with a faint smile and hurried from the room, sensing that she had intruded at an inopportune moment, wondering what would be the final outcome of the young woman's sojourn in the house. She had her suspicions — but she did not voice them even to her crony, Jeffries . . .

Kyre regained his composure and moved to the tray to pour the coffee. Sara managed a faint smile as he passed her cup to her and then sat down in one of the deep armchairs.

'I think I shall always associate you with coffee,' she said as lightly as she could.

He looked up, an enquiry in his eyes. 'That sounds as though you mean to leave, after all.'

She nodded. 'I haven't changed my mind. I know you think it will be difficult for me to work and care for Adam — but I shall manage.' There was pride in her voice.

'Of course you will,' he agreed but there was sadness in his heart. 'I shall miss you,' he added abruptly.

She glanced at him in surprise. 'You haven't seen very much of me,' she reminded him.

'Enough to know that I shall miss you,' he told her quietly.

Faint colour stole into her face. 'I expect we shall meet again. After all, you and the others are the only family that Adam has . . . apart from Simon and he seems to be settled abroad. I think children should grow up with all the advantages that a family can offer.'

'So do I. That's why I wish I could persuade you to remain here,' he said firmly. Then, an ironic smile playing about his mouth, he added: 'Although there won't be much family here for him to grow up with, it seems. My sister and her husband are going to look for a house of their own. Cathryn and Kane are going to be married . . . so that only leaves myself and the older generation.'

'I thought your brother and Cathryn would live here when they married,' she pointed out swiftly.

'So did I . . . but circumstances have changed. Cathryn will probably live in London — and I expect Kane will live wherever his wife chooses. The old order changeth . . . '

'You don't seem to mind.'

He smiled. 'No, I don't think I do. Perhaps my outlook is becoming less medieval, Sara. I don't think one can cling to the ways of the past — not successfully. I realise now that Melanie and Philip should have been encouraged to make a home of their own years ago. The house will seem empty at first, of course — and I shall miss the children. There have always been children in this house.'

She looked at him curiously. 'One day

your own children will fill the house, Kyre. You will have a family of your own. The house won't seem empty, then. And I should have thought you would prefer to be on your own with Honor when you're married . . . '

He interrupted her quickly: 'Honor? We aren't going to be married, Sara.'

Her heart leaped with sudden, bewildering hope. 'You're not . . . ?' She stilled the words abruptly, hoping that she had not seemed too pleased, too eager.

'No. Honor is marrying my brother. Very soon, I believe.'

'Kane? But I thought . . . I was told . . . don't you *mind*, Kyre?' The words tumbled out impulsively.

He smiled at her — a secret, intimate smile. 'To be frank, I'm vastly relieved. I've never wanted to marry Honor — and never had the courage to say so. Kane has solved that problem for me.'

'Then I didn't misunderstand? It was generally assumed . . . ?'

'Oh, yes. People have been expecting

me to marry Honor for years — even Honor herself. But I think she's quite happy about the outcome. So you see, I shall be virtually alone in this big house — and, I admit, rather lonely. Uncle James and Aunt Dimity are a wonderful couple — but scarcely congenial companions for a man of my age.'

Sara met his eyes with the undeniable, unmistakable appeal in their depths — and her heart missed a beat. Perhaps she was leaping to conclusions . . . perhaps he was merely concerned for her welfare and the problem of Adam . . . perhaps he was moved solely by his innate kindness and generosity. Yet surely there was more than kindness, more than generosity, more than concern in his dark eyes? Surely there was the hint of genuine affection, of heart-warming interest — and even the promise of love, she thought with a catch of her breath.

She did not know if the strange, sweet emotion she knew was the dawning of love in her heart. She did not know if the future could bring a balm for her bitterness, an ease for her loneliness, a new joy to her life in the safe harbour of this man's arms. She did know that she did not want to leave the house that she had hated so much until this moment, that she did not want to leave this man whom she could trust and respect — and possibly love with all her heart . . .

'Kyre . . . ' She said his name shyly, uncertainly, even tremulously.

He took her hands and drew her towards him. 'Will you stay, Sara? Will you allow me to look after you, to help you with Adam, to . . . love you a little?' His smile was very sweet, his eyes warm with tenderness, his hands gentle and reassuring . . . his smile pierced the last barriers of resistance, his eyes looked long and deep into her own and his touch moved her to a flood of thankful emotion.

She nodded without speaking — and he raised her hands one by one to his lips. She raised her face to him and he kissed her gently, fleetingly — his kiss was the promise of happiness to come and the key to a new and shining future . . .

THE END